MW01519730

# DAUGHTER OF THE NIGHT

TIKI KOS

Edited by
PINPOINT EDITING

This book is a work of fiction. Names, characters, places and incidents are the product of the author's imagination or are used fictitiously. Any resemblance to actual events, locales, or persons, living or dead, is coincidental.

Copyright © 2016 by Tihana Kos

All rights reserved. The scanning, uploading and electronic sharing of any part of this book without the permission of the Author is unlawful piracy and theft of the author's intellectual property. If you would like to use material from the book (other than for review purposes). Prior written permission must be obtained by contacting the Author at tiki_14a@hotmail.com

ISBN-10: 099591110X

ISBN-13: 978-0995911109

*This book is for anyone who has lost faith. This is proof if you just believe in yourself for one second, you can accomplish amazing things. This is for the lost, the found, and everyone in between. Just believe!*

# CHAPTER ONE

AFTER A LENGTHY SHIFT AT THE STEAMING MUGS CAFÉ, SERENA took her usual shortcut through Avonmore Park. Walking off the path into the pine trees, she tripped over a pile of rocks scattered across the grass. She stood back up, brushing the dirt off her jeans. In the distance she could hear low rumbling whispers. She whirled around, looking for a clue of where the noise was coming from. All she could tell was that it surrounded her. When she turned back around, shadowy figures crept out of the darkness. A crowd of men in matching brown robes made their way towards her, chanting. Some held weapons and others had books with swirls of weird symbols.

*"Daughter of Nótt, your sacrifice will bring the end. Daughter of Nótt, your sacrifice will not be in vain."*

Running towards a small opening between the men, she tried to slam her body through the encroaching intruders.

"Let me go!" Two men grabbed hold of her wrists, twisting her arms and overpowering Serena down to the ground. As the attackers squeezed, tightening the grips on her wrists, Serena squinted, forcing herself to focus on the intruding faces. Instead of eyes, they had hollow, empty holes, and mouths full of rotting teeth. The smell of rancid flesh slithered its way up into her nose. She could taste the bile rise in her throat. Her stomach twisted and turned; she tried to turn her face away but, no matter what she did, the smell followed.

One of the men strolled out of the circle, bending down next to Serena. Lifting her red shirt to expose her stomach, he pulled out a jagged silver knife and pushed the tip deep into her flesh. Serena felt a warm stream of blood trickle down the side of her ribs.

"Stop! Get off me!" The man ignored her pleas and continued to drag the dagger across the edges of her skin. Bucking both her legs and attempting to twist her wrists, Serena let out a banshee-like scream.

She sat up.

She dragged the air into her lungs, releasing it in relief. She could feel the sticky sweat building up on her forehead, and wiped at it with her pajama sleeve. "This nightmare is going to be the death of me."

Trying to shake off the night's event, Serena flipped on the radio.

*"Police are investigating the strange and sudden death of hundreds of magpies. Last night, at around 5pm, witnesses say the birds suddenly stopped flying and fell to the ground. Avonmore Park will be closed as the investigation continues."*

Rummaging through the overstuffed closet, she finally found the red Steaming Mugs t-shirt and slipped it over her head. She matched it with a pair of dark blue jeans, pulling them over her voluptuous curves.

Serena found her favorite pair of red flats against the wall. As she put her feet inside, she inspected the worn shoes. The bottom soles hung on by just a thread and the red was rubbed off, exposing the brown underlay. She loved these shoes; they were the last gift from her mother. "It's almost time to retire these babies." She rubbed a smudge of dirt that painted the side of her shoe. "I really should get a roommate or a cat so I can stop talking to myself."

The radio anchor continued. *"Now on the line, we have one of the country's top ornithologists, Dr. Heather Mayfair. Now, Dr. Mayfair, what could be some causes for the strange occurrences?"*

A soft voice began to speak. *"Events like this have happened across the world. In most cases, the weather is to blame. Often, it's caused by lightning or high altitude hail. Until I receive a sample, I won't be able to know the exact cause."*

Switching off the radio, Serena stretched both arms into the air and let out a yawn. There hadn't been a storm the previous night; she would have woken up.

Entering her small bathroom, she brushed the knots out of her long, chestnut brown hair, and lazily tied it up into a bun. Digging through her makeup bag on top of the counter, she pulled out a tube of mascara. She ran the wand through her eyelashes, making the contrast between her blue pupils and black lashes pop. The ringing of the grandfather clock in the living room reminded Serena that it was noon.

*I'd better go check on Marbles. I'm going to be late for work if I don't hurry.*

Trotting down the stairs and out the front door, she crossed the lawn, the dewy tips of grass brushing against her feet. Every once in a while, Serena had to cat sit for her elderly neighbor, Mariah. Mariah often visited her children, who lived a couple of hours away in the small city of Langley.

Unlocking the door, Serena was greeted by a fluffy white and grey cat. "Hey Marbles, are you hungry?" Serena asked, rubbing the tabby's furry back. Purring and meowing, Marbles lifted his paws and swiped down on top of Serena's hand. Small oozes of blood appeared. "Ouch! Don't use your claws when you're happy to see me."

Marbles followed her down the hallway into the kitchen. Serena poured a mountain of kibble into the cat's bowl. The tabby rushed to it and shoved his face deep into the food.

Serena rubbed him on the back. "I'll see you later. I can't be late for work. Don't claw me again," she pouted. Inspecting the claw mark, she wiped the blood against her pant leg.

Serena Annar had grown up in the small serene town of Avonmore. Avonmore was built in the center of a huge pine forest, with most of its residents working in the neighboring lumber mills. The main street was one large circle surrounding Avonmore park, which was the center of the ongoing magpie mystery.

Continuing along the main street on her way to work, Serena paused when she passed a building in the midst of being torn down. It had once belonged to her family. There, in the middle of the dirt lot, stood heavy machinery, tools, and construction workers scattered all around. A neon sign flashed *Coming Soon: Avonmore Mall*. Every time Serena walked past the lot, she would get lost in memories, her mother's soft voice ringing through her head. At times, she could see her mother and father standing in the dirt, edging her on to come with them, but then if she moved even an inch, they would disappear.

A car horn sounded obnoxiously; the smell of burning rubber filled the air, followed by the crunching sound of metal, snapping her out of the daydream. Her body jerked up; she covered both ears and closed her eyes tightly. There was a flash of the night of the accident: the moment of impact and the overpowering smell of gas mixed with burning tires.

Two years ago, her family had been on their way home from the company Christmas party. Their car hit black ice; spinning out of control, it drove into oncoming traffic. Both parents died instantly, but Serena miraculously survived with a couple of broken bones and a bad concussion.

She wiped a couple of warm tears away and hurried down the street to the café, humming a little tune as she tried to shake off the bad memories. The panicky feeling from vehicles happened too often for comfort and in this moment,

Serena was thankful that she could walk everywhere in the small town.

As soon as she walked into the café, she was comforted by the smell of freshly brewed coffee and baked cookies. Her nerves slowed down and she felt as if she could breathe again.

"You look completely exhausted. Did you even get any sleep?" Her manager Jeremy shook his head at her disapprovingly. Jeremy had buzzed-off red hair, long gangly arms, and a crooked smile. She'd been working for him for the past two years, and he was the closest thing to a friend she'd ever had. Serena sighed; she hated this question more than she should.

"I was studying for my college entrance exam, and then it happened again."

His wild red eyebrows frowned. "Same dream as always, hey?"

Jeremy poured a big splash of coffee into a red mug and handed it to Serena. She quickly downed the drink.

"Thanks. I already had a rough start today with the nightmare and Marbles. The little bugger clawed my hand."

Jeremy scanned Serena's hands, his forehead crinkling in confusion.

"I don't see anything."

Serena glanced down. Jeremy was right—her hand looked as though nothing had happened. Tying the apron around her waist, a loud beep came from the oven across from the coffee machines. She slipped on some oven mitts and pulled out the metal baking sheet full of sizzling oatmeal cookies. Jeremy placed some wire cooling racks on top of the counter next to the oven.

"You know, maybe it's time to talk to someone about this dream. I mean, it can't be normal to have the same one every night for two years."

Serena shrugged her shoulders. "I have no idea what people do in this type of situation. I don't know how I really feel about opening up to a complete stranger. They might just put me in the looney bin and throw away the key."

"I doubt that would ever happen." Jeremy placed a hand on top of her shoulder. "You know, I can come over sometime after work and help you look." She placed the steaming cookies on top of the cooling racks.

"Maybe. I just need to think about it for a while. I'll let you know if I need any help." Jeremy went into the back room and grabbed his backpack. He poured himself a coffee and grabbed an oatmeal cookie. "You just let me know if—or when—you want help. Oh, and I won't forget that you have the rest of this week off. Good luck studying for your exam, and I'll see you next week."

Serena nodded, giving Jeremy a quick wave goodbye. She liked Jeremy, but he tended to ask her the same questions over and over. *What do you want to study in college? Do you want to work at a coffee shop for the rest of your life?* The moment her parents died, Serena threw out any plans of school or life. She was coasting and really didn't mind serving coffee. She enjoyed the free refills and baking; that was her mother's favorite pastime.

❦

After a busy day making cookies and coffee, Serena looked up at the clock. *Could this day have dragged on even longer?* She flipped over the *Closed* sign and wiped down all the tables and counters around the shop. Throwing the used cloth back into the sink, she went into the back room to grab the broom and started sweeping the floor. *Is it really that weird that I have the same dream every night? I guess it wouldn't hurt to talk to someone. I could just go to one appointment and see if it's for me.*

Making sure all the appliances were turned off, she grabbed her keys and headed out the door, locking it behind her. She quickly glanced at the clock through the door. *It's already nine? Time to book it back home.*

She cut across the Main Street and headed towards Avonmore Park. Bright blue police barricades blocked her usual shortcut. *How could I forget about the investigation?* Taking a sharp right, she detoured towards the small local theatre and church. Avonmore was not a busy place in the evenings, with only one pub in town and most of the stores closing at eight. An older couple was sitting on a bench in front of the church, holding hands and whispering secrets into each other's ears. *So cute…to be that much in love when you're that old…*

High school boys on skateboards were hanging around the blocked off entrance to the park, trying to dare each other to go inside. Serena was shaking her head towards the boys and yelled a little louder than she should. "I'm pretty sure you don't want to go see all those dead birds and maybe catch whatever freaky disease they have."

The boys laughed in her direction and Serena could have sworn she heard one of them whisper, "Paranoid." Distracted by the boys, wanting to see if one would be brave, Serena bumped into someone.

Without looking up, she automatically responded. "I'm so sorry, I wasn't paying attention."

She followed the length of the body from bottom to top, meeting with a face she never thought she would truly encounter.

The man had hollow black eyes, a crooked grin, and jagged teeth. Serena's heart began to beat faster and faster— she swore if it went even faster it would jump right out of her chest. She launched her body past the man, running into the high school field. In the middle of the field, she stopped, trying to catch her breath to stop her pulse from jumping around sporadically. The sides of her body throbbed. She thought this might be the time she needed to start going back to gym. The air around her seemed to thicken and her body trembled from the cold. Goosebumps rose from her arms, and she just knew *something* was behind her.

Serena whipped around in fear to face a dark figure. The shadow moved fast, coming closer and closer. Serena wanted to move, she really did, but her body disagreed and froze in place. To her relief, the shadowy creature finally hit a street light, exposing her supposed attacker. Serena laughed nervously. "Hey, little buddy." The golden retriever ran towards her, rubbing his furry body all over her dark jeans. She patted him on the back. An older man rushed to the dog's side, holding a leash in his hand.

"Miss, are you all right? You seemed like you saw a ghost when you bumped into me back there." She let out a small chuckle, scanning his seemingly normal features.

"Yes, thank you. I'm very sorry, my mind was playing tricks on me." She patted the dog one final time and headed up the street to her house, shaking her head while she walked up the stairs.

"I can't believe that just happened. Jeremy is right; I must be losing my mind."

Serena ripped off her work clothes, which now had the bitter smell of coffee. She pulled open an overstuffed drawer and took out a pair of pink fuzzy floral pajamas—she had more pajamas than she would like to admit. She pulled out her laptop and flopped down on the bed.

Opening Google, Serena searched for therapists near Avonmore. After looking at a few websites, she found a couple in Langley. "Better make an appointment. Somehow, I don't think it's normal to hallucinate..." Serena let out a big yawn and placed the laptop on her nightstand. "I need to get some sleep and put all this craziness behind me."

The moment she closed her eyes, a loud screech came through the open bedroom window, followed by what sounded like glass crashing down on concrete.

*What kind of trouble did Marbles get into now? Now that I*

*think about it, I completely forgot to feed him after work.* Serena quickly threw on a purple robe and a pair of matching slippers. She grabbed her keys from the nightstand and headed to Mariah's house.

Rushing to open her neighbor's door, she turned on the front entry lights. "Marbles? What did you do? I hope you didn't break one of Mariah's ceramic dolls or her vases. She is going to be so angry!" She peeked in the living room to see if she could find the tabby cat.

"Serena, is that you?" Mariah's voice came from upstairs. "Please, Serena, help me; I'm up in my room."

Thinking Mariah must have fallen, Serena went up the stairs and slipped into the bedroom. Mariah sat on a chair in the middle of the room, bound by rope.

"Oh thank God, Serena. When I came home, a man came up from behind me and forced himself in. He attacked me and dragged me into my room!" Serena rushed to Mariah's side, fumbling to undo the ropes.

"Mariah, where did the man go?"

Mariah shook her full head of grey hair. "I don't know. His cellphone rang and he just left." Marbles ran into the room, hissing and screeching at Mariah. His white paws were dirty with splatters of blood.

"Marbles, what did you get yourself into? We need to get Mariah out of here and call the police." Serena picked up the tabby and petted his head to try to calm him down. "Shh. It'll be okay."

Mariah wrapped her wrinkled arms around Serena. "Thank you. You keep an eye on the door, and I'll try to find my phone to call the police." Serena nodded.

Mariah rummaged through the room while Serena peeked through the bedroom door down into the hallway. "What did your attacker look like?"

Mariah's voice sounded raspier than usual. "Some young punk with black hair. Thought he could overpower me."

Serena frowned. "What? Why would he break in? Maybe money? Or do you have something extremely valuable?"

"You stupid, annoying human. He broke in because I killed this useless meat bag." Mariah's voice rumbled as she let out a manly growl.

*Meat bag?*

Whipping around, Serena watched Mariah rip the flesh off her face strip by strip and fling the excess skin on the ground.

Serena tried to move her legs, but they wouldn't cooperate and began to tremble instead.

"What the hell is going on?"

Underneath the skin, there was a mutated dog face, and Mariah's body was completely covered in dense black fur. Her hands transformed into humongous crooked claws. Slobber oozed out the creature's mouth as it snapped its large, jagged teeth at Serena.

"With all that meat on you, you're going to taste so good."

Serena pushed her legs to run down the stairs, holding onto Marbles. She made it halfway out the front door before a large claw dug into her shoulder, pulling her back into the house.

The creature climbed on top of Serena, pinning her body onto the ground. Marbles flew out of her hands, landing on all fours. He jumped onto the creature's face, digging his claws in deep into the black fur, trying to wrap his small little jaw around any part he could. The creature continued to hold Serena down with one claw, grabbed the tabby with the other, and threw him against the wall.

With one last weak *meow*, Marbles stopped moving. Serena lifted herself off the ground and wrapped her mouth around the creature's arm, biting as hard as she could.

"Don't hurt Marbles, you freak!" Serena spat, blood and fur landing on the carpet.

The creature snorted. "Like that would hurt me."

The creature bent down and licked her neck. Slobber

dripped down the side of her face. Slowly sinking its own teeth deep into her neck, the creature ripped off a chunk of flesh.

Serena screamed as blood shot from the wound, a wave of the warm liquid soaking her pajama top. The scent of blood seemed to excite the creature, and its mouth panted. The panting became ragged and quick as it dug its crooked claws deep into both of her shoulders. Serena's head spun, her rapid heartbeat slowing down. Tears rolled down both cheeks; her mouth had the faintest taste of copper and bile. *I'm going to die.* She lifted a numb arm, wrapping fingers around the creature, trying to pry it away. Without any effort, the creature flicked her hand. Her arm flopped to the ground like it was made of putty.

"You are going to be one tasty main meal."

Barely able to keep her eyes open, Serena looked past the creature's blurry face. An outline of a man appeared behind the creature. His blurry body lifted what looked like a sword in the air and swooshed it down, pushing the weapon through the creature's back. Her ears rung as the creature let out a deafening bellow. The tip of the sword exited through the chest, the heart still attached.

The room continued to spin as Serena's eyes began to roll backwards.

The last thing she saw before passing out was two violet eyes.

# CHAPTER TWO

A CHILL PASSED OVER SERENA'S BODY AS SHE SLOWLY REGAINED consciousness. Her eyes gradually opened up to see a dark concrete ceiling with cobwebs hanging from the corners. Of course, in this moment, the old wives' tale of people eating spiders in their sleep popped in her head. The thought of spiders crawling over her body made her shiver; she shook her head and snapped back to reality.

"What? Where am I?" She sat up, only to be pulled back down by rough metal shackles. "What the hell is going on?" Serena looked around the dimly lit room. She was imprisoned by thick metal bars, and lit candle torches were hanging from the walls. "What is this, the Stone Age?" Goosebumps made the hairs on her arms rise. Serena started to yell. "Somebody get me out of here! What do you think this is? I have rights!"

The shackles tightened as she squirmed to pull her wrists out. From down the dimly lit hall, a handsome man, no older than 20, with black curly hair and familiar violet eyes, came towards the bars.

"You have been detained by the Einherja. No human has ever survived an attack from a skin walker. What kind of demon are you?" He opened the lock to the cell and walked towards Serena.

She shook her head. "Demon? I'm just an eighteen-year-old barista from Avonmore." Serena gulped. She could feel her palms begin to sweat and her heart pound. All she wanted to do was crawl back into her bed and forget about the evening's events. "Listen, I did nothing wrong; I just want to go home. I promise I won't tell anyone what happened. I don't know anything about 'demons' or 'skin walkers'."

The man chuckled, shaking his curls from side to side. "Who do you think I am? I'm not going to fall for that. I don't know if you know the rules, but the punishment for breaking the Ragnarok Treaty is imprisonment or death. No demon is allowed entrance to Midgard. As I said, no human has ever lived through a skin walker attack. It's only been four days and your 'fatal' wounds are almost healed. That just isn't possible." *What the hell is he talking about?* He gently pulled the shoulder of her pajamas down. "See for yourself."

Serena followed his gaze to see only faint red marks and freshly pink skin.

"It always seems to happen if I get hurt or sick; it just goes away quickly." The man's eyebrows furrowed.

"This is a trick."

Serena shook her head. "This isn't a trick. I just want to go home. Please, I promise I won't tell anyone about you or the 'demons'. I just need to go and call the police. I was attacked and my neighbour was killed by a maniac."

The man placed his hand over his forehead and let out an exasperated sigh. "You were attacked by a skin walker. How many times do I have to say this?" *He's delusional.*

"Please don't murder me…" Serena squeaked.

A deep voice came from behind the man.

"A skin walker is a demon who consumes the skin of its prey and gains the ability to transform into whomever it has killed. If a human is attacked by a skin walker, they are cursed. The next full moon, they transform into a demon. This is why he is asking what you are." The beautiful man had golden hair and eyes that reminded Serena of the ocean. "I am Dawn, and this is Justice. We are the Commanders of this Sanctuary. We are the protectors of Midgard—Earth, as you call it. You were attacked by a demon, and Justice thought maybe you were one also."

Justice removed the shackles from her wrists. Puffy red welts rose from the indents, which she gently rubbed. Both legs tingled as she pushed her body off the concrete slab. *This is a good sign. If they wanted to kill me, they would have kept me shackled, right?*

"My name is Serena Annar. I live in Avonmore. I'm sorry to disappoint you, but I am no demon." Justice lifted his hand above Serena's face.

"Maybe we should try a truth spell?"

Serena snickered. "A truth spell? Is this some sort of LARPing game? Is Jeremy playing a prank on me?"

Both boys looked at each other.

Dawn finally turned towards Serena.

"What is LARPing? And what is Jeremy?"

"Jeremy is human." Serena bit down on her lip. "LARPing. Live action role playing game. You know, you dress up in costumes and pretend to fight dragons, elves...fantasy creatures. Listen, guys, you two are amazing actors, but I'm just not into this kind of stuff. I really need to get home and study. How did you get Mariah to play such a terrible joke on me?" Serena rubbed her sweaty palms against her blood-stained pajama pants. "I know her son is a drama major in college, but this is just plain mean. Was is it because I didn't want to go on a date with him?"

Justice placed a hand on Dawn's shoulder, and they both started laughing hard. Dawn wiped a couple of tears from his eyes and tried to catch his breath.

"You ramble a lot, and what you said does not make

sense. This not a game or an elaborate joke. Everything you have witnessed was real. How could anyone fake what you saw? Plus, you were injured very badly. You were in a lot of pain."

That was true; no one could ever orchestrate such an elaborate prank.

She nodded in agreement and bit down on her lip. "But demons can't be real. There's no way…people would freak out and the government would intervene and kill them. Right?"

Dawn pulled the cell door open. The hinges squealed like fingernails on a chalkboard. With a flick of his finger, he motioned for Serena to follow.

"How can you be so certain? I would like to show you something. I know this is a bit frightening for you, and overwhelming. But please, Serena, just follow us. I promise, if you are not comfortable, you can go home right away."

Serena crossed her arms and frowned. "I'll go with you, but just so I can go back home and have a scalding hot shower." *Should I make a run for it?* When Serena stepped out of the cell, she glanced both ways. She had two options: follow the boys, or go the opposite way, which was unlit and made her stomach feel uneasy. *Nope!*

She followed the boys into a dimly lit hallway. A row of cells stood on either side as they continued to walk through the hallway. Serena tried to sneak a glimpse of what was in each one. *What would they need all these for?* In the first cell, Serena made eye contact with a young boy with elongated ears poking through his silver hair. Then, she walked passed a man who was at least eight feet tall, with a slightly disfigured face. A putrid smell of dung and sweat crept through the cell; Serena couldn't help but crinkle her nose.

The prisoner waved his shackled hand as her mouth slightly opened and she stopped to stare. *Don't gawk, Serena.* She whispered an apology to the giant man. His neighbor was a huge humanoid green snake, wearing a ripped brown cloth around its waist. *What the hell is that?*

The snake hissed and revealed a long, red split tongue.

A pale woman with long, curly bronze hair came towards the cell bars. Her smile revealed two protruding teeth.

"Come closer..." Her voice felt like velvet to Serena's ears. Without a thought, she started to walk towards the cell. Justice grabbed Serena's arm, pulling her back. He quickly waved his hand in front of the woman.

"*Stilne.*" The women's lips were moving, but not a single sound could be heard. Serena watched as she banged on the cell bars in silence.

"How did you do that?"

Dawn stood beside Serena, pulling her towards the wall. "It was a spell. You should not get too close to the cells. Any one of these creatures would attack you without hesitation—especially that filthy blood sucker."

They continued in silence, making their way up a rickety wooden staircase.

At the top of the stairs, they entered a spacious dining room. Dawn shut the door. He waved his hand and whispered, "*Låse.*" Serena jumped as a loud click came from the door.

"What did you do?"

Dawn turned towards her. "It was another spell to lock the door in case the prisoners somehow escape."

In the middle of the room stood a long wooden table covered with glass cups and ceramic golden plates. A beautiful burgundy rug with gold trim covered the entire floor. She walked towards the wall, which had several paintings of men and women fighting enormous creatures. Examining each one, she ran her fingers over the golden frames. Everything about the room took her breath away.

One painting stood out more than the others. It covered the entire ceiling, portraying a magnificent castle of gold surrounded by the clear blue waterfalls and a giant lush forest. The sky twirled with a blend of oranges, pinks and purples. A rainbow bridge connected the golden castle to the planet Earth.

"I've never seen so much gold before. Or a rainbow bridge. Whoever painted it must have had a vivid imagination." One by one, everyone in the room followed Serena's gaze up to the ceiling. Justice traced the edges of the rainbow bridge as her eyes couldn't help but follow.

"That is Asgard, where the Aesir Gods used to live. Asgard was once connected to Earth by that rainbow bridge —Bifröst. The way to Asgard has been lost to our people for centuries."

*Gods? This is so surreal.*

"Like Asgard as in Thor and Odin? They couldn't be real, right?"

Dawn's blue eyes flickered in amusement. "They were real once upon a time."

Dawn went through a wooden door across from the table. He came back out carrying a bottle of water. He handed it to Serena, giving her a toothy grin.

Serena hastily took a swig, the cool liquid soothing the nagging in her throat. "I really needed that. My throat feels like I've just come back from the desert."

Dawn gestured for her to follow him through another door.

As they continued down a golden washed hall, they finally entered an enormous gym. The smell of blood and sweat tickled Serena's nose. Soft blue cushioned mats covered the entire floor. Hanging on the walls were an assortment of weapons—Serena could only guess that there were several hundred of each. One wall was completely covered in a thick beige rope net, and various gym equipment was leaning against the opposite one.

A young blonde girl with elongated pointy ears and light

orange skin ran towards Serena. "Hey girl! I'm Aimee; it's so nice to have another female around here. Welcome to the Avonmore Sanctuary." She smiled sweetly and had a pleasant demeanor that calmed Serena.

"Thanks, Aimee. I'm Serena. Have you lived here long?"

Aimee nodded her blonde wavy hair. "I have been here since I was fourteen...So it has been four years." For a moment, Aimee and Justice locked eyes, lost in their own world. Swirls of pink washed over the elf's round cheeks. Serena felt like an intruder watching the quick exchange.

Aimee turned to her and gave her the brightest smile. "Come sit with me at supper, Serena. That is, if you decide to stay." Serena nodded. "I'll see you guys later." In the corner of her eye, she saw Justice wink at Aimee.

He grinned watching Serena's reaction. "She happens to be a very powerful sorcerer as well."

Serena felt awestruck. "Your lives are like a real-life video game. Powerful sorcerer elves and mystical creatures. Save the earth from evil. Jeremy would be very jealous of me right now. He's an avid Dungeons & Dragons player."

Justice's disapproval clearly showed on his face and the edges of his smile pulled down. "I wish it were a video game. Just press *restart* when someone dies. Unfortunately, this is our life. We all have abilities that make us stronger and able to heal faster. But we are not invincible. We can grow old and get killed."

Dawn placed a hand on top of his friend's shoulder. "Or die by getting eaten by an old hag like the Onibaba. Erik was unfortunate to encounter one on his sixteenth birthday—it jumped out at him right in the middle of the forest."

Serena watched as Justice's posture sprung up straight, his chest puffing out. He reminded her of one of those exotic birds from the amazon trying to impress a suitor. Justice rolled his lips, slapping down on Dawn's hand. "That old hag had no chance against my brother." His features softened he turned towards Serena. "Erik is my older brother; he runs this Sanctuary. I think he is one of the most powerful Einherja that ever was. He is very blessed by Odin."

"I didn't know anyone still believed in Odin." Both boys ignored her comment.

They reached the end of the hall and entered a crowded library. Books were stacked all the way to the ceiling. They seemed to be endless. *How long have they been collecting them?* Serena walked towards a wooden shelf. She blew off the dust to read the titles. *History of Demonology? The Rise and Fall of Surtur? Odin's Conquest?*

"I've never heard of any of these books. The Avonmore library has never stocked anything about demons before." Serena pulled out a demonology book and flipped through the stained pages. A musty smell touched her nostrils. "Succubus?" She began to read. "A demon in female form that appears in dreams and seduces men."

On the bottom of the page, a faded picture had a naked winged woman with a serpentine tail hovering above a man who was asleep. She slammed the book shut and shoved it back on the shelf. Serena closed her eyes. *I will never be able to erase that picture.* Justice stood next to her. His violent eyes twinkled in amusement. "How could all these creatures exist without anyone finding out about them?"

Justice shrugged. "There have been humans who have seen demons. How do you think they came up with supernatural books and movies? Most people just brush it off and think it is their mind playing tricks. Some people tell others and it becomes an urban legend. Most of the creatures and demons in urban legends and mythology are real. Every type of culture has a different god and evil beings. They are all real. It is not just Aesir gods that were alive."

She thought about it for a minute. "How are there real gods and demons just running around the world. It just doesn't make any sense."

Justice shook his head. "Well, they are not technically 'running around the world'. Most have their own realms or dimensions. It would be impossible to even know if any of the other Gods are alive now. Their dimensions are not connected to ours."

"Still not helping." Serena rubbed the temples of her forehead. "This is weird. Are any Aesir gods still alive?"

"Not many. Most are just descendants."

Justice pointed towards a winding staircase on the other side of the library. "Up those stairs are all the bedrooms and bathrooms." *Disney would go crazy for this house.*

Serena watched as Dawn blew off the layers of dust on each pile of books. "I will just be a minute; I need find *The Chronicles of the Night*." Justice followed behind Dawn, sifting through some overlooked piles. After a few minutes, Dawn pulled a leather-bound book from the wooden shelf. He rubbed the book against his shirt and placed it on top of the wooden table. Serena pulled out a creaky chair and sat down beside the boy.

Dawn hummed to himself as he flipped through the pages. He cleared his throat and began to read. "Nótt's second marriage was to a mortal man named Annar, resulting in a daughter called Joro. Nótt's first husband, Dellinger, learned of the marriage and vowed to punish Nótt. He tried to poison Joro and kill the mortal man. To protect Nótt, Odin placed her in the sky with her chariot and her horse Hrimfaxl. To punish Dellinger, Odin placed him in the sky at dawn to chase Nótt, but to never be with her again. Every 24 hours, they race through the skies.

"Serena, you are a descendent of Nótt, the Goddess of the night, and this is why you are unaffected by the skin walkers' curse. Odin placed your path to meet ours. You are meant to be at the Sanctuary and train to become an Einherja. You are chosen." *Into every generation, there is a chosen one. She alone will stand against the vampires, the demons...*

"I am also a descendent of Nótt. My family are descendants of the god Dellinger. I guess you are part of my family." Dawn's face lit up.

*A descendant of a goddess?* Justice's lips drooped. "She already has a job being a barista. She might not want to put herself in danger." Justice pulled the book towards him and flipped through the pages. "Plus, you must have a life you want to get back to in Avonmore. Serena might not *want* to train as an Einherja."

*You just told me I could be like Buffy. This is a 90's teenage girls dream come true!*

Dawn turned towards Serena. "Also, we will have to see what Erik says when he comes back from the Elder meeting."

She shrugged nonchalantly, trying to slow down her voice to hide the excitement. "I *guess* I could try to train with you. I'm not sure if I'll be any good. Plus, my life isn't anything special right now. I'm pretty much alone most of the time. I really don't know if I'll be capable to train. I barely work out as it is."

*I didn't really want to go to college just yet. Do I really want this to become my life? Hell YES!*

All three of them left the library and went back into the hallway. Her stomach rumbled loudly and she rubbed it to soothe the hunger pains.

"I guess we should go eat some food. Follow me, Serena. You must be starving from not eating for four days." Dawn gently took Serena's hand and guided her back to the dining hall.

As they walked back into the dining room, Justice and Aimee's eyes locked back onto each other's. He gave her a quick smile, slightly bowed his head, and sat at the opposite end of the table. Dawn sat down beside him and started whispered in his ear. Aimee was engaged at the table with two teenage boys.

"Serena, come sit with us and meet the boys." Serena sat

next to Aimee and introduced herself to the others. There was a curly redhead boy, Gamble, a fifteen-year-old sorcerer from Vanaheim. He stood up and offered Serena his hand. He waved his hand and whispered *"Bloomstre."* A pink daisy manifested out of thin air. *What? That is so cool!* Serena began to get giddy as she took the flower. Next to Gamble was Aidan, a light blue skinned elf with dark blue spikey hair from Alfheim.

Serena smelled the flower as she lifted it up towards her nose, and she asked how long the boys have been living at the Sanctuary.

The boys took a minute to answer. Aidan counted the months. "It has almost been one whole year."

Serena grabbed a pitcher of water from the table and poured it into her cup. She took a big gulp; with everything they'd told her, she might need a stronger drink. "So...how do people end up coming to the Sanctuary?"

Aimee looked at Serena. "It depends. Often Einherja are chosen by the Elders or High Councillor for having extraordinary skills. It is a great honor. At times, they are chosen if they are orphaned and have no other family to take care of them. Most Einherja only stay at the Sanctuary until they turn thirty; then, they move onto other jobs or start families. I was chosen for my magical aptitude, as was Gamble."

Aidan softly spoke. "My parents died, and I had no other family. The High Councillor of Alfheim sent me to join Aimee." Serena wanted to wrap both arms around the boy and not let go. She could see the pain in his eyes, the same pain she recognized when she looked in the mirror. He must be close to her own age when her parents died.

"Sooo...how many realms are there?" Serena tipped her head to the side. "We are on Earth, or Midgard, as Dawn called it. Vanaheim is where most of the Sorcerers and Elders live. Alfheim is where the elves live. Is Asgard even a realm?

If no one can find it or even if they did, it's forbidden to enter. Am I missing any others?"

Gamble nodded in agreement. "Those are some of the realms. But I think Asgard is not quite a realm. It is more like a spiritual plane. It's not of this world, existing beyond the horizon, out of the reach of any demi gods or descendants."

*What?*

Serena's head throbbed she tried to make sense of everything.

Aidan turned to her and whispered. "It's okay to be confused. No one understands what Asgard is anymore. It's been lost to the descendants of the Aesir gods for so long, it's just a myth now. Who knows if it really existed? There are so many theories."

Aimee turned towards Serena. "Asgard has been the topic of great debates for as long as we can remember. But I have a theory that it still exists; someone just needs to find a way to unlock it. The gods must have a plan. They wouldn't leave such a powerful place untouched for so long."

Gamble pushed a dinner knife into the table and carved a giant tree. "So to make it less confusing, we will count Asgard as a realm. In the eighth century, there were nine total realms." Asgard, Vanaheim, and Alfheim were carved into the top of the tree. Midgard, Nidavellir, and Jotunheim into the middle. Svartalfheim, Niffleheim, and Muspelheim were carved into the bottom.

After the uprising, Nidavellir, Jotunheim, Svartalfheim were destroyed." He slowly waved his hand above the table. "*Forsvinne.*"

The carving disappeared and table top looked brand new. Serena's eyes went big.

"Very impressive magic skills, and a lot of information to think about. My brain feels a bit jumbled." She ran her hand over the table where the carving had disappeared. Aimee giggled and turned towards Serena

"Don't worry. In no time, all of this will just feel like your normal life. Magic, demons and training will become second nature to you."

"Hmmm...I'm not sure if I will ever get used to being a descendant of a god, or knowing that magic is real."

Two elderly dark grey skinned elves with black hair came into the room with trays of food and pitchers of water. Serena stood up and placed the pitchers of water on top of the table. "Thank you so much for all this wonderful smelling food. Are you both from Alfheim also?" The elves looked down at the ground, shook their heads, and scurried back into the kitchen. Serena stared at the fleeing elves.

Aimee smiled. "Dark elves are usually very skeptical when they meet new people. Often, they are mistreated and don't want to become too casual with the wrong person from the wrong family." Aimee explained that the dark elves had gone against the gods in the Ragnarok War, resulting in the destruction of the dark elf realm of Svartalfheim. Due to the treaty, all dark elves became slaves or were banished to the underworld, Muspelheim.

After eating stir fry vegetables with chicken and a bit too much chocolate cake, Serena was full and exhausted. She felt like she could sleep off another four days. "That was ridiculously good. I haven't had such good cooking in a long time."

"The Bloodrose's are notoriously great cooks. Would you like to pick out a bedroom, Serena?" Serena nodded, and the two girls made their way upstairs. "Well, you *only* have about fifty to choose from."

Serena picked one in the farthest corner, overlooking the wild flowers and with a view of Avonmore in the distance.

"Aimee, how is it possible that I have lived in Avonmore my whole life and I have never heard of this mansion?"

Aimee leaned against the wall. "There are powerful wards protecting the house from any humans or creatures. The house will never be seen unless it wants to be. If you leave and want to find your way back, on the left side of the highway next to the first sign to Langley, there is a huge pine tree that towers all the others. This pine tree has a beacon spell on it, so it always looks like it's flashing to any Einherja. Go through the pine trees until they become weeping willows. As you follow the weeping willows, you come to the edge of the flowers and say '*Oppstå*'. The wards will recognize you."

*Oppstå. Don't forget.* "Thanks again for everything."

Aimee gave Serena a quick hug. "It's not a big deal. I'm just so excited to finally have another girl here. It's boring with all these boys; all they want to do is play video games and fight each other. I will see you tomorrow, lady." Serena nodded, watching Aimee walk down into the hallway. *I guess I shouldn't tell her I love playing video games.*

A wooden chair stood near the window, overlooking the back yard. In the corner of the room was a closet and bathroom. Serena splashed hot water over her face and tried to scrub away the crusted blood. *The gods must be wealthy!*

She shrugged, and a wave of bitter odor filled the room. *Phew! I need a shower.* She stripped off the blood crusted pajamas and threw them down next to the bed. Goosebumps rose over her body. Her head pounded and all Serena wanted was a good night's rest. She crawled into the bed, tightly wrapping herself up in a fur blanket.

*Could this whole day be one messed up dream?* Going over the day's events, she finally closed her eyes and drifted off into a deep sleep.

*Serena walked into Avonmore Park. She abandoned her usual path to walk into the pine trees, and tripped over a rock. Looking down at the rocks, she noticed they were meticulously placed into the shape of a pentagram. Awaiting the arrival of the robed men, she turned to see a woman with bronze skin drifting towards her. She was surrounded by long graceful hair the color of the night sky, and had ember eyes.*

*Serena squinted to see what the woman carried around her neck. As she came closer, there was a sickening smell and a tapping noise.*

Tap, tap, tap.

*Frozen with fear, Serena was finally able to focus on what was around the woman's neck: severed hands and feet, tapping against one another. Her mouth was smeared with bright red blood.*

*She lunged towards Serena, grabbing her arms. As she tried to pull away, the woman's arms turned to rotting flesh, and maggots were crawling out of her dress. Laughing, the woman bent down and kissed her, Serena could feel the maggots drop one by one into her mouth.*

*"Daughter of Nótt, your sacrifice will not be in vain."*

Serena felt two hands around her shoulders.

"SERENA, WAKE UP!

# CHAPTER THREE

Serena jerked her body up, trying to spit the maggots out. "Ah, that was so gross!" Her shoulders relaxed as she let out a sigh.

A calm voice came from the corner of the bed.

"Are you doing okay?" Serena's body lifted a couple inches off the bed, her heart beating like a drum. Her mouth dropped and she slowly nodded her head. A beautiful man with wispy black hair just past his ears, dark, violet eyes and a strong jawline sat on the bed. Those violet eyes watched her intensely. As the shock wore away, she could feel a surge of blood run through her cheeks.

"What the hell? Who are you? Were you watching me sleep?" Serena looked down at her chest and quickly pulled the fur blanket around her naked body.

Her face started to burn as if it were on fire, and she covered her eyes with her hands. *No one has ever seen me naked before.* He slowly pulled both hands away from her face

"It's okay, Serena. I heard you screaming from my room. I just wanted to see if you were safe." Serena shook his hand off.

"I'm not going to lie to you; this is a little creepy."

He lowered his gaze, inspecting his bright blue shoelaces. "Sorry, I am not trying to be creepy." He slowly raised his head up, both eyes locking with Serena's. "I am Erik Baldr. I am the Guardian of this Sanctuary."

Her voice became shaky. "Well, it's nice to meet you, Erik. I'm Serena. Sorry you had to meet me when I was naked."

Erik's cheeks turned pink as he cleared his throat. "It's not a problem. I didn't see anything." Serena scrunched both eyebrows while she glared towards him. *Yeah, I doubt that.* He fiddled with his thumbs to avoid her glare. "So, I hear you are the descendant of Nótt. My brother, Justice, and Dawn have filled me in about your situation. This past week I have been in Vanaheim in a meeting with the Elders. I'm sorry to hear about you finding out about your ancestors in such a violent way." Every time their eyes met, the violet seemed to spark brighter.

"At times, the veil between the realms becomes weak, allowing lesser demons—like the skin walker who attacked you—to walk the earth. This is part of our calling as Einherja. We protect the earth and try to keep the demon population to a minimum. There are several Sanctuaries across the world, filled with descendants of the gods and elves."

"You're like secret agents protecting the earth from villains that are demons and vampires and weird snake people." Serena nodded. "Einherja." Oh God, the word vomit had begun.

Erik's laugh rolled over her like the ocean waves. "Yeah. You could say that."

He handed her a worn grey sweater and black sweatpants. "Justice told me you didn't have a change of clothes, so I thought you might like a sweater and a pair of pants for now."

As she slipped it on, the smell of cinnamon danced through her nostrils. *God, he even smells good.* "Erik, it's fascinating that there is this whole entire hidden world—pardon me, *worlds*—and so much history no one even knows about."

Erik's face beamed as Serena talked. *Stop acting awkward.*

Underneath the blanket, Serena pulled the sweatpants over her shaking legs. "I'm not sure how long that dream would have lasted if you hadn't woken me up." She ran a hand through her knotty hair. "Every night for the past two years, I've had the same nightmare. In this dream, I was waiting for it to happen as it always does, but instead, this weird rotten flesh woman appeared and attacked me, filling my mouth with maggots."

With the mention of maggots, he squirmed around the bed and his nose crinkled up. "No wonder you were screaming. I really hate maggots."

"Right? These dreams are so real, I feel like I am supposed to be doing something about it. They feel like warnings. *Don't go in the forest, you're going to get murdered.*" Erik's eyebrow arched, and he ran a finger against his stubbly chin. He thought about what she'd said for a couple of minutes.

"Perhaps, if you have been having them for the past two years. The descendants of Nótt have been known for having premonitions when they are dreaming. Some have been able to see into the past as well. Nótt flying through the sky seems to amplify your bloodline's powers."

*Marvel is going to make a movie about my life. 'Super barista saves the planet with powers that only work when she is sleeping'.*

"Before this whole mess happened, I thought I might be going a little crazy. I almost started to believe that my mind was punishing me for living while my parents died." Serena shrugged. "I guess it was a good thing I found out I have superpowers. Well, not that Mariah died and I got hurt, but...you know what I'm trying to say. It's never good when people get eaten by a werewolf thingy..." Serena covered her eyes with her hand. "Sorry, sometimes I just babble a lot. Especially when I'm nervous. I call it word vomit."

Erik shrugged, keeping a straight face. "I am glad I was here to help, and if you ever need someone to talk to, I am here for you any time—day or night. It becomes overwhelming at times when all these strange things start happening to you and you don't fully understand why." He handed her a large, worn book. "After these confusing couple of days, I figure you would like to learn more about the Ragnarok War and treaty. As Guardian, some of my responsibilities are to oversee that every Einherja is properly trained and educated. We can start on your training in a couple of days if you would like. Please, try to get some rest." He patted her shoulder. "I can tell you will be a refreshing addition to the Einherja...even with the word babble."

Erik gave her a quick wink as he smiled brilliantly and left the room. *Whoa, what a cute man.* Serena let out a giddy laugh. "Is it too soon to have a crush?" She waved a hand over her hot cheeks "I need to pull myself together and stop acting like a fan girl. But I can only imagine what his abs look like under his shirt." Eyeing the leather-bound book, she ran a hand over the smooth, soft cover. "I don't want to visit that freaky dream again, and I should really stop thinking about Erik."

Serena wrapped herself with the blanket and sat down on the comfy wooden chair near the window. Nothing smelt as good as an old, musty book. She began to read.

"The Battle of Ragnarok took place in Asgard. Loki, with the support of the giants, dark elves and dwarfs, led the attack against the Aesir Gods. After, he killed the God Baldr and took the golden horn. Loki was angry that he was cast out of Asgard by Odin to live eternally in the underworld. Loki crossed the rainbow bridge that the God Heimdall guarded. He stormed the gates with all the manpower of all the lower realms."

Serena put down the book and looked up at the sky. For a minute, she could have sworn she saw Nótt flying in her chariot. Feeling comforted by this, she fell into a deep sleep.

A loud knock echoed through the room.

"Just a minute." She wrapped the blanket tightly around her shivering body, before opening the door to see the two elderly elves. The woman had the brightest smile Serena had ever seen; the man was more reserved, dodging her glance.

"Miss, we retrieved some of your belongings from your house, and this creature followed us back to the Sanctuary." The older male elf dragged in a trunk, placing it next to the closet. Marbles leaped between the elves into Serena's arms. "Oh Marbles, I'm so sorry." Serena hugged the tabby and snuggled her face deep into his soft fur.

"Also, we thought you would enjoy some lunch." The elderly women gently put down a tray of vegetables and sandwiches on top of the window sill.

"Call me Serena. Thanks for the lunch and for grabbing some of my clothes. I was beginning to smell weird—like sour yogurt."

The male elf offered a wrinkly grey hand, gripping Serena's and giving her a strong shake. "It's nice to meet you, Serena. I am Nathaniel Bloodrose, and this is my wife, Milia. We have served the Baldr family for the past fifty years." Milia offered her own and gave Serena a much softer shake.

"it's really nice to meet you both." Milia's grey skin crinkled as she grabbed the soiled clothes. Nathaniel pushed open the bedroom door, turning one last time towards her.

"The Guardian wishes to see you in the library when you are ready." The elves smiled and took their leave.

*And I wish to see him, too—shirtless*, Serena laughed to herself.

Marbles curled up on the bed and fell asleep. As Serena finished eating her lunch, she burrowed through the leather trunk. She grabbed some capri leggings, a baggy orange sweater, and some flats.

Walking down the stairs into the library, Serena heard giggling and some books falling. There, sitting on a pile of dusty books, was Justice kissing Aimee. Quietly, Serena tip toed around to the other side of the room, before walking into the corner of a table. "Ouch!"

Justice and Aimee quickly back away from each other. Aimee's orange skin turned a deep red as she fumbled to button up her shirt, "Justice..." He ran out of the library without a whisper.

"Oops! I didn't want you to see me, but why did he run away? It's really not a big deal."

"Justice and Erik's father is an Elder; he doesn't want his precious bloodline tainted with another elf. Justice is worried he will find out.

"Before the war of Ragnarok, the elves and gods never really got along. Some of the older families still look down at elves and treat us like trash. They think because their descendants were gods they are better than everyone else. People are scared of how wild and uncontrollable elven magic can be."

Serena rolled her eyes. "Unbelievable that people could think like that. Really? How long has this been happening?"

Aimee sighed. "We have been secretly together for a couple of years. I truly love him with all my heart. Unfortunately, his father insists that he marries this stupid ditz, Nina. She just wants to marry him for his money and to be part of an Elder family. Every couple of months, his father and Nina come for a visit. It's so awkward—they throw this big supper and no one even talks."

Serena wrapped both arms tightly around the elf and squeezed. "Have you tried to talk to Erik about it?"

She lowered her face, playing with her fingers. "No, we haven't talked to Erik, but I think he has always suspected we are together. You don't know Henrik Baldr. He is a very powerful man with many powerful friends."

Serena really didn't want to know him.

She lifted Aimee's chin up. "Listen to me, Aimee. We won't sit around and let Justice marry ditzy Nina—I promise. This will be our secret, and we'll think of a plan." Aimee's face lit up and Serena winked at her.

Erik walked into the library, wearing a tight long-sleeve black shirt that outlined his muscular arms, and carrying two cups of coffee. Serena couldn't help but stare at his muscles and his beautiful violet eyes. As he passed her a cup, all she could smell was cinnamon and nutmeg, making her head feel a little dizzy.

"It's time for your magic lesson outside. Aidan and Gamble are waiting for you."

Aimee waggled her blonde eyebrows at Serena. "I will see *you* later." She rushed to the door, giving the duo one last look over before leaving.

"Coffee!" Serena took a sip of coffee, the chocolatey nutty flavors danced around her taste buds. "Everyone is so great here. I forgot what it felt like not to be lonely."

Erik nodded. "I understand how you feel. After my mother killed herself, this place was the only thing that kept me together." There was such sadness in his voice, Serena wondered how awkward it would get if she just wrapped her arms around him.

He pulled out a piece of paper from his pocket and handed it to Serena. "This is what she wrote before she died. *His mouth is full of cursing and deceit and fraud: under his tongue is mischief and vanity–Psalm 10:7.* I keep this as a reminder of how much I need the Sanctuary. Without it, I have nothing." Serena wondered if she should ask him about his father, but pushed that thought out of her mind.

"When did she die?"

He sighed and looked down at his feet. "I was 15. I had just been appointed the youngest Guardian of a Sanctuary, I remember my mother was so happy, and when I left, she took her own life." Her body shivered; she wasn't sure if it was cold or from Erik talking about his dead mother. She wrapped her arms around herself.

"I know it doesn't seem like it, but you're very lucky you had the Sanctuary and Justice." She lowered her eyes. "When my parents died, I was old enough to get emancipated. I was alone in their house and I only left to go work at the café. I was in a very dark place, surrounded by the reminder of them."

Erik's eyes locked on to Serena's. "Justice and I buried her in this beautiful forest in Alfheim. She loved all the elves and the magic that pulsed through the air. It was her haven."

Serena memorized Erik's features on his face, the dimples when he spoke of his mother. *And those piercing eyes. I can't seem to get over them.* "Can I ask you a question?" Erik nodded his head. "This might sound weird, but how do you and your brother have violet eyes?"

He ran a hand through the wispy black hair. "My mother Ailsa was part elf. Violet eyes run in her family, and I am thankful every day that I have a reminder of her."

She flashed him a wide smile. "I think your mother would be so proud of you. Justice is lucky to have such a wonderful older brother keeping up this Sanctuary and protecting Avonmore. It's a big responsibility. I know I just met you, but I think you're doing a great job.

"I want to stay here with you. I mean, I would really like you to train me." Erik's face lit up while his violet eyes glimmered.

"Well maybe we should just start your training tomorrow morning. I will meet you outside your door." That was music to Serena's ears, she still was exhausted and didn't really feel like doing much.

§

After an uneventful sleep, Serena sat up in bed and stretched out both arms. Her shoulders felt better than they had in a long while, as if the weight of the world had been lifted. She smiled as Marbles made soft whistling snores.

*That is the first time in two years without being unconscious that I've had no dream.* She threw on some black leggings and a long sleeve t-shirt, before kissing the tabby and heading out the door. Erik waited for her in the hallway.

Serena perked up. "Good morning!" He handed her a chocolate chip oatmeal muffin. *He brings me food. He is gorgeous. There must be something wrong with him — I don't think anyone can actually be this perfect.* "Delicious. Would you like half?" Instead of waiting for him to reply, she took a huge bite into the crumbly muffin.

He shook his head while he let out a laugh. "You just ate more than half the muffin in one bite. You didn't even give me a chance to answer."

She finished off the muffin and tried to muffle a laugh. "Well, you were too slow and I love chocolate. Next time, you should just bring another."

Erik's lips tightened. "So you think there will be a next time after you ate the whole entire muffin without sharing? Chocolate chips happen to be my favorite."

She nudged his side. "Well, I thought Einherja were supposed to be super-fast and strong."

"You're right about that." He burst out laughing. "Next time I will be faster and take a bite right away."

Nodding her head, she giggled. "You won't be fast enough; no one gets between me and chocolate."

"I accept your challenge, Serena Annar."

They both laughed and talked about trivial things while Serena followed Erik down into the gym. He instructed her to take off her shoes and stand with her legs shoulder width apart. He grabbed two small silver swords off the wall and handed one to her.

His grip tightened on the sword. Even without moving an

inch, he looked so graceful and natural. "Try to hit me with your sword, and don't hold anything back."

Serena dashed towards him, but the sword was heavier than she thought. "Uhh..." Lifting it as high as she could, with great effort she swooped it down, barely grazing his own. As he blocked her attack, it flung across the room against the wall. Serena paused, watching the weapon lie on the floor. *Buffy would be shaking her head and laughing at me.*

"Not bad for someone who hasn't used a sword before. Let's try it again. Get back into position." Erik handed the sword back to her and laid down his own. He came up from behind and wrapped his muscular arms around hers. In this moment, Serena could swear her face was bright red.

"You need to hold your hilt harder."

Serena muttered softly, "Okay. I will." He squeezed her hands. She could feel the warm breath tickling the small hairs on the back of her neck.

"Try to always keep your hands this tight." He let go and picked his sword back up. "Again." She lifted her sword up, thrusting it towards Erik. As he blocked her attack, this time the sword barely moved an inch. "Bend your knees slightly. Stay in that stance. I am going to attack you. Ready?" She nodded. He swung the sword. The sound of metal clashing together echoed through the gym. "Good. Always remember that stance; it will be harder to knock you down.

"Let's try something different." Erik pointed towards the wall covered in a thick rope net, which reached to the very top of the ceiling. She rubbed both hands together, then wrapped one after the other around the stiff rope. Ripples vibrated her arms as she pulled her body off the ground. She placed a foot on top of the rope. To her surprise, Serena managed to reach the middle. Looking over her shoulder, she glanced down at Erik. He stood so causally with the most charming smile. His eyes were glued to her. A sour taste filled her mouth.

*Oh shit! Why did I look down?* Her heart began to race and both hands felt clammy. Her stomach twisted and turned as if it were on a roller coaster.

"You are doing great, Serena. Take a deep breath and don't look down again."

Erik moved closer to the rope. "You can come down if you don't feel comfortable."

She nodded. "You're right. I'm coming down." Serena lowered her foot. She missed the rope and tumbled. Trying to pull herself up, her arms gave out. Serena let out a loud shriek as she fell. A loud thump filled the air as she landed right on top of Erik. He burst out laughing.

"It's okay. I got you. I think we are finished today."

Serena's sides throbbed from the uncontrollable laughter. "I hope I didn't hurt you."

She stood up, offering Erik her hand. He wrapped his fingers with hers as she grunted, pulling him to his feet.

"I am not hurt at all. Well, maybe my ears a little. You know how to shriek; you must have some banshee in your blood." She pressed her lips together at Erik's deep chuckle. "I would really like to show you something tonight. Is it all right if I come get you from your room around eight?"

*Is the Pope Catholic?*

Serena beamed happily, trying to hide the excitement in her voice. *YES!* She wanted to squeal—and loudly.

Erik shook his head while he walked towards the door. Before leaving, he turned around to look at Serena. "You know, Serena, you are really something else."

She heard him laughing all the way down the hall. Sitting down on the blue cushion, she rambled to herself. "Is it weird to like someone this fast after meeting them? I will have to talk to Aimee next time I see her. She did say she was in love with Justice when she first saw him. No, it shouldn't be that weird."

Dawn walked into gym, holding a piece of paper. "Were you just having a conversation with yourself?"

Serena stood up quickly. "No. I have no idea what you are talking about." He continued across the room, giving her a shifty look.

"You're a little weird." She shrugged her shoulders and bit her lip to hold in a giggle.

"I am." *I wonder how gossipy Dawn is?* Serena doubted he would go around telling everyone the new girl liked talking to herself.

Serena headed to the kitchen to see if the dark elves were around. When she walked through the door, her eyes grew bigger. *I can't believe the size of this place.* The kitchen was the biggest she had ever seen. Two large ovens were side by side, next to stainless steel fridges. In the middle of the room was a wooden island filled with drawers. She ran her finger against the speckled golden marble counter tops. *This is every baker's dream kitchen.* Milia was near the ovens, checking on a roast while gravy bubbled in the pot on top of the oven. Nathaniel was sitting down on a wooden stool peeling potatoes; he tossed them into a pot on the island.

"It smells so good in here." It made her stomach rumble in hunger.

Both elves were startled to see her. "Miss Serena, is there something you need us to do?" Milia softly smiled while she whisked her gravy. Serena shook her head.

"No, I was just wondering if you wouldn't mind if I baked some chocolate chip cookies. I really want to surprise Erik. Do you think you have the right ingredients?"

Nathaniel put down his knife while he stood up from the stool. "Of course, Miss Serena. Follow me to the pantry." He walked towards a door across the kitchen. "Everything you need should be on one of these shelves."

Serena smiled. "Thank you, Nathaniel." The pantry's shelves were fully stocked. After five minutes of searching for the baking shelf, she gathered up all her ingredients and began to bake some cookies.

The two dark elves went on to tell her about their children. Their two youngest sons were serving Elder Henrik Baldr in Vanaheim, and the two older daughters serving the High Councilor in Alfheim. Twice a year, they went to visit the children, and were are able to send letters whenever they liked. Serena bent down and looked into the small glass oven window to check the cookies. "What is Henrik Baldr like?"

Milia scoffed. Her usual smile soured and the lines on her face scrunched. "He is a cruel and intolerant..."

Nathaniel cut her off. "Milia, you know better than that. If Master Henrik ever found out what you said, he would punish our family greatly." Milia quickly looked down continued to whisk the gravy.

"That was rude. I really shouldn't have asked that." Milia opened one of the island drawers and pulled out a metal wire rack.

She placed the rack on the counter next to Serena. "Vanaheim is a beautiful realm. They have many statues and temples dedicated to the Aesir Gods."

Serena sat down on the stool next to Nathaniel. *I see Henrik is a touchy subject for a lot of people.* She picked up a small knife and began to peel potatoes. "How do you get to the other realms?"

Nathaniel piled a bunch of potatoes on top of the counter. "In each Sanctuary, there are usually two portals: one in the front entry and one in the attic."

"What about the people who don't live in Sanctuaries? How do they get to the other realms?"

Milia grabbed the filled pot next to Nathaniel. "In both capitals, there are multiple portals. Some powerful sorcerers are able to create a portal out of nothing."

Serena was impressed. While she finished off the potatoes, the oven let out a loud beep. She pulled out the cookies, placing them down on the rack. Once they were cool, she placed half on a plate and left half for the elves. "Thanks for the company."

Nathaniel nodded. "It's not a problem, Miss Serena. It's not often we get visitors in the kitchen."

She smiled at the elderly elf. "Well, you will definitely see more of me. The kitchen is my favorite place to be."

Serena picked up the plate of cookies. "Milia, could you please show me where Erik's room is? I would like to leave him these." Milia nodded as she headed out the door, Serena following closely behind.

"Of course, Miss Serena. I don't mind at all."

Milia took Serena to Erik's room, which happened to be right across from her own. "I am so sorry for asking about Henrik. I really shouldn't be so curious; I don't want you to get into any trouble."

"It isn't any bother at all. The Baldr boys are a wonderful sort. They take after their mother, Ailsa. Beautiful, kind soul, she was. She would always treat my family as equals. As do the boys. But, Miss Serena, stay away from Henrik. He doesn't take too kindly to outsiders—especially ones who take up with his sons." Milia rubbed Serena's arm. "He despises anyone with elf or human blood."

Serena frowned. *What is she trying to tell me? I'm not going stop liking Erik, even though his father's a horrible person.*

"Miss Serena, if that is everything, I need to finish making supper." Milia scurried off down the stairs.

Serena gently knocked on the door. "Erik, are you in there?" She waited for a few minutes for an answer.

Opening the door a crack, she placed the plate full of cookies down on the ground. *Hopefully he won't step on them and ruin my surprise.*

# CHAPTER FOUR

When Serena entered the dining room, supper was already spread out. She grabbed a plate and filled it to the rim. She tapped her foot impatiently. *Stop being so nervous. He probably just wants to teach me something about being an Einherja. This is not a date...*Her hunger got the better of her and she dove into the mountain of meat and potatoes. After the plate had not even a crumb left, she took her dish back into the kitchen. The digital clock on the stove flashed to seven thirty.

Nearly falling up the stairs, she ran into her room to get ready. In a haze of panic, she picked out a short dress with flats. *This should do the trick!* Combing her knotty hair, Serena realized she really needed to go home to grab the rest of her stuff—including her hair straighteners. She braided her hair off to the side. She sat down in the hallway, the cool hardwood floor easing her shaking legs. Erik strolled out of the room, eating the cookies with smeared bits of chocolate around his mouth, wearing a black button down shirt and dark jeans. *He reminds me of a young Bruce Wayne.*

Erik offered her a hand and pulled her up onto her feet. "Milia told me you baked these cookies. You're beautiful, and a talented baker." Serena smirked and lifted her finger against his cheek. She wiped the chocolate off his face.

"And you, Erik, are a disaster." Erik gave her a goofy grin before he inhaled the rest of the cookie. "My mom taught me how to bake when I was little. I know some of her recipes by heart now."

Erik gently wrapped his fingers around Serena's and walked towards the end of the hallway, where they reached another set of stairs. "I guess I am a pretty lucky guy to have you bake for me. Has anyone shown you the attic yet?" Serena shook her head, each step creaking one by one until they reached the top. Erik held the door opened for her as she walked through.

"Why thank you, kind sir." She bowed her head down. "Such a gentleman." Every space in the musty attic was occupied with either books or table top glass display boxes.

She walked towards the tables and peered down into the displays. "What are all these things?"

Erik followed, and pointed to the first display. "That is the tip of Loki's Staff." Serena followed his gaze to see three large golden spikes with a glowing blue crystal floating in the center. "Each Sanctuary stores important items from the war, or anything the councils would like to protect."

She ran a finger against the glass display, a trail of dust following. "Don't try to open the displays, though They have powerful wards protecting them. Only Guardians are able to handle the items." Erik ran his hand against the glass.

"There was this one time when a vampire prisoner escaped. He tried to grab Loki's staff." He snapped his fingers. "Poof. He was on fire in an instant. Man, do those vampires burn quickly."

She jerked, taking her finger off the display. "I wouldn't want to see anyone on fire. Ick."

Erik nodded. "It wasn't a pretty sight." He pointed to the last display. "Here is the tunic my ancestor Baldr died in."

Serena walked towards the display, looking down at the deep blue tunic. It had a beautiful golden circlet belt wrapped around the cloth. "But these boring relics are not what I wanted to show you."

He walked towards the giant metal arch in the middle of the room. "Do you know what this is?" He ran his hand up the arch, tracing the swirled carvings.

Serena shrugged. "Did you buy a prop from *Stargate*? Looks like what they use to go to different worlds."

A grin crossed Erik's face, and he softly chuckled. "That is pretty close; it's a portal. I want to take you somewhere. The first time always feels a little strange, but don't be afraid. I won't let anything happen to you." He waved his hand in front of the arch. "*Åpne veien.*" A bright blue swirling light appeared in the middle of the arch. It swayed like the ocean waves but never spilled out. Erik gently took her hand and they walked together through the portal. "Don't be scared." Serena felt as if a vacuum was trying to suction her very soul.

Frightened that she would let go and get lost, Serena squeezed Erik's hand as hard as she could. At the very end of the blue light, a golden door stood, surrounded by green, leafy vines. Erik grabbed hold of the vine handle and pulled the door open. They both walked through the door into a humid forest. Serena looked at the bottom of her braid as the ends curled. Erik let go of her hand and shook his around.

"Wow, what a grip you have. I am lucky my hand didn't fall off." Serena rolled her eyes.

Erik lifted his hands up in the air. "Welcome to the beautiful realm of Alfheim, home to the elves and Fae." The forest floor was completely covered in a blue green moss unlike any Serena had ever seen. Flowers of every color grew everywhere the moss missed. Little bright balls were dancing through the sky and bounced off the giant oak trees. Serena could hear little whispers and giggles surrounding her. Erik gently caught a ball and opened his palm to show her. "It's a

Fae. They protect the forests and animals all around Alfheim."

Serena bent down, taking a closer look at the Fae. "She is so cute. Can they understand us? Can I *keep* her?" The Fae bowed her head down towards Serena and stuck her itsy bitsy tongue out. She had shimmering silver skin and purple butterfly wings. The other Fae flew down, pulled the petals off the flowers and started to sprinkle them all around. Serena twirled around in the falling petals. She grabbed onto Erik's hands, forcing him to join her. She burst out laughing while the forest continued to spin. "I'm dizzy!" She stopped and released Erik's hand, her head continuing to spin. *I haven't spun like that since I was a kid.*

Erik brushed the petals off Serena's face and tightly wrapped his arms around her waist. He pulled her closer as he leaned in and softly brushed his lips against hers. His lips tasted like cinnamon. Erik lifted her up and gently laid her down on the soft moss, his warm body covering hers. He brushed a stray hair from her face behind her ear. Serena swore her face felt as if it were on fire.

"The minute I saw you, you took my breath away. I haven't been able to think of anything else."

"Really?" Serena laughed. "I thought you might think I'm a little too weird."

"You are weird." His violet eyes flared, and his lips met Serena once again. "But I like it. You make me laugh." As Serena began to answer, a group of giggling Fae sprinkled white dust above the couple. The group quickly flew away as the dust created a cloud, which engulfed Serena and Erik.

Snoring loudly, Erik lay down next to Serena, snuggling his head on top of her shoulder. Serena yawned as her head slowly fell to the ground. She started to mutter, "I feel the..." She tried to jerk awake but the warmth of Erik's head lulled her to sleep.

🦋

Sometime during the night, the Fae had wrapped the couple in a blanket made of moss and flowers.

Serena looked down to find herself standing on a dark cloud in the sky. "What's going on? Why can't I feel my body?" She giggled as the stars swirled around her and wisps of air tickled her sides. A soothing *neigh* filled the air as a black horse with the darkest mane she had ever seen pulling a black chariot came racing to her side. The horse rubbed its mane against her cheek. Serena gently embraced him. A beautiful woman with skin the color of the night sky and shimmering silver hair embraced Serena.

"My beautiful daughter—the night will protect you. I am Nótt, and I will forever be by your side." She smiled, running a hand down Serena's braid. Serena wrapped her arms around Nótt.

"Thank you. I wish I had known about you before." Nótt kissed the top of Serena's forehead. "Don't worry, child. We have plenty of time to know each other." Nótt put her hand through Serena's chest. Serena gasped, her eyes winced watching the hand go through her chest. She could only feel the smallest little spark of energy. Nótt pulled out a small black dagger. "My heart will become your heart." Serena felt a warm hand on her shoulder.

"Serena...wake up." Erik plucked the moss out of her hair, and ran a finger against her cheek. "Those Fae like to play tricks sometimes. Last time, they stole my watch and shoes. You should check if they stole anything from you. They really like shiny things." She shook her head. "I don't think they stole anything from me." As she sat up, Serena felt a small prick on her arm. There on her lap sat the dagger Nótt had pulled out of her chest. While she began to wrap her hand on the hilt, a glowing word appeared. "*Natt*...what does that mean, Erik?"

He thought about it for a minute. "I am pretty sure that means *night*. Where did you get that dagger?"

The carved word disappeared as Erik reached for the hilt. "Nótt came to me in my dreams and said the night would protect me." He handed the dagger back and it lit up again in her hands.

"You are truly blessed, Serena Annar." He stood back up and pulled Serena back onto her feet. "We should be getting back to the Sanctuary. I need a coffee." Serena grabbed his face and kissed him hard on the lips. Her head started spinning again from his cinnamon taste. She whispered into his ear.

"I really like you too, Erik Baldr. I just wanted to clear the air." Serena cleared her throat. "Coffee sounds perfect right now." The corner of his eyes crinkled as she spoke. He held out his hand towards her.

"Ready to go back?"

She nodded, wrapping her fingers around his "Only if you promise we can come back sometime."

Erik smiled "Of course. We can come back whenever you would like. This is my favorite realm. Next time, I would love to show you the capital city, Eldamar." They held hands while they walked through the portal into the blue light.

# CHAPTER FIVE

ON THEIR RETURN TO THE SANCTUARY, THEY HEARD VOICES AND crashing from the library. Serena frowned, studying Erik's face. "What's going on?"

Erik shook his head. "I don't know, but I'd better go check it out." He dropped Serena's hand and shuffled down the stairs, her following shortly behind. *Why did I wear such a short dress?* Erik was racing towards an older man, yelling at him. Once Serena reached the bottom step, she held on to the banister, taking a deep breath in. Droplets of sweat came rolling down her forehead and a burning sensation filled her lungs. *God, I need to work out more.* In the corner of her eye, she saw Erik pull a dagger from his belt and point it towards an older man who stood above Justice.

"Father...stop." Justice lay motionless on the ground, crumpled in a ball, his face bloody and freshly bruised. Aimee wrapped her arms around him, rocking him back and forth. "Wake up, Justice. I need you to wake up." Her eyes were puffy and bloodshot. Erik pushed his father away, creating a wall between the two.

Henrik shook his bloody fist towards Erik. "How could you let this happen, Erik? Your brother believes he will marry this filthy knife ear. Couldn't even be a man to tell me himself." Henrik wiped the blood from his knuckles onto his white shirt. "You will do no such thing, you hear me, Justice? I will not have my only two sons ruin our legacy." Henrik pulled a hand through his salt and pepper slicked hair. He walked around Erik towards Serena, leering at her with his dark green eyes. "And who might this pretty little thing be?" He ran a finger down Serena's face, and she stepped back.

"I am Serena, descendant of Nótt."

He sneered at her. "Nótt, that pathetic woman stuck in the sky. Your sad little family once had a seat with the Elders but were kicked off. You are the worthless half-breed offspring of Selina...nothing sadder than a god marrying a measly human."

"I would rather be a human than a complete asshole. Look at what you've done to your family." The vein in Henrik's temple throbbed. He tightly wrapped his hands around Serena's neck.

"You think you can talk to an Elder like that? Maybe I should teach you a lesson in manners."

Erik pried the hands off her throat, and Serena rubbed her fingers around her neck while she gasped for air.

With both hands, Erik shoved Henrik, slamming him into a bookshelf.

He jabbed his dagger against Henrik's throat. "Don't you ever touch her again!"

Henrik laughed, glaring at Serena. "I see; another woman trying to turn one of my sons against me. First your mother, then the knife ear, and now this little half-breed. I will not forget this."

Erik pushed his dagger in a little deeper, slowly cutting into Henrik's throat. "Get out. You are not welcome here."

"You're not so scared of me anymore, boy. You're finally growing some balls." As Henrik made his way back into the hall, closely followed by Erik, he turned to wink at Serena. "I will see you very soon, Daughter of Nótt."

Aimee tried to lift Justice off the ground, but almost instantly dropped him. Her hands become shaky and the tears continued to fall down her face. Serena lifted one of Justice's arms and wrapped it around her shoulder, Aimee grabbing the other. Serena turned towards her. "Ready?" Aimee nodded.

In one swift motion, they pulled his body up. Taking one step at time, they finally made it up the staircase. Serena's arms tingled and shook. Except for the occasional grunt, neither girl said a single word until they reached Aimee's room and placed the motionless Justice on top of the bed. Aimee sat down next to him, brushing her lips against his still cheeks. Softly, she pushed the bloody curls off his forehead and with one finger traced down until she reached his heart. Her voice whimpered and shook. "Please, Justice. Just open your eyes and wake up. It's that easy."

Serena's eyebrows furrowed; she couldn't help but to stare at Aimee's shirt. It had missing buttons and the seam frayed. She sat next to her friend and gently rubbed her back. "Aimee, tell me what happened."

She sniffled, wiping her nose on her sleeve. "I was reading in the library when Henrik came up behind me. He said a courier dropping off supplies had heard us talking about getting married. He pushed me against the table and started to tear my pants off, so I screamed and Justice came running from the training room." Aimee buried her face between her hands. "Justice pushed him off me and punched him in the face, but Henrik got back up and just kept punching him. He didn't even stop when he passed out." Serena wrapped her arms around the elf and squeezed as hard as she could.

"Don't worry; Justice is a fighter. He will wake up."

"I really hope so."

Erik and the dark elves stumbled into the room, carrying

supplies. Milia filled a bowl with hot water and wiped the blood off Justice's face, while Nathaniel started to stitch up the wounds. After each wound was closed, he then rubbed green herbs over the stitches. Then, they placed green candles around the room. Aimee walked towards the center of the room, and waved her hand, "*Sparke*," igniting a wave of bright blue flames on each candle.

Erik placed his ear on top of Justice's chest. "His heart is beating out of control." He waved his hand above his chest. "*Hele*." Erik listened again. "That is much better."

Nathaniel and Milia joined hands with Aimee, created a circle.

> "*Danu, mother of all, lend your power.*
> *Bring Justice peace this very hour.*
> *I call upon your strength and might,*
> *bless your child this secret night.*"

Aimee leaned down and kissed Justice on the forehead before lying next to him and grabbing his hand. "There is nothing left to do but pray to the gods and wait. I think it would be best if you all left."

Serena pulled the blanket over the couple. "Please let me know if there is anything I can do."

She gave Serena a slight nod. "I will."

Erik leaned down and kissed his brother on the forehead. "Be strong, brother." He squeezed Aimee's hand quickly before he headed out the bedroom door, Serena following him.

"Erik..." She tried to reach for him, but he jerked his arm away from her hand.

"I can't do this right now, Serena." Without another word, he disappeared down the stairs.

*I am sorry, Erik.* Exhausted, Serena slumped down in front of Aimee's door and, without any effort, dozed off.

❧

The next morning, Marbles came running down the hall and crawled on top of Serena's lap.

"Marbles, yesterday I had one of the best and worst days ever. What am I going to do?" He let out a loud *meow* in response, before scurrying down the stairs. "Hey, where are you going?" Serena chased after the tabby until he finally stopped in middle of the gym, rolling around on top of the mats. "You are right; I should train." She went to the shelf where Erik had pulled out the sneakers. Underneath was a pile of workout clothes with leather straps placed on top. *Perfect.*

Looping the leather strap around her body, Serena then buckled the belt tightly around her waist and slipped Nótt's dagger into it. "All right, Marbles, let's pick out some other weapons." She found a small sword that fit perfectly into the sheath, and grabbed another dagger for her belt.

Serena stood with her legs shoulder width apart and practiced drawing her sword. *From making coffee to practicing with swords. Barista to demon slayer. Jeremy would be so proud of me.*

Finding its placement on her back awkward, she took off the sheath and placed it back into the cube, deciding to practice with the training dummy instead. She pulled out her daggers, jabbing them into its side. "Take that, demon dummy." Serena ducked underneath the arm, pulling out the daggers. She kicked the dummy in the back and dug her blades back in.

Loud claps and a small cheer came from the doorway.

"Congratulations! You have officially killed that dummy."

Dawn strolled into the room, wearing a grey sweat suit. "I am glad to see you're practicing; would you like some help?"

She nodded. "I want to be prepared for anything." Serena smiled and wiped the sticky sweat off her forehead.

Dawn set up some wooden blocks around the room.

"Okay, I want you to run and jump over the blocks. Then, on the way back, I want you to climb over them."

Again and again, Serena stumbled over the blocks, growling unintelligible sounds. Each round, Dawn made the blocks a little higher. She wasn't sure how long her body would hold up against them.

Without a complaint, she managed to finish the training. Serena never really knew anything about Dawn. She was actually surprised he wanted to help her; he had barely acknowledged her since their first meeting. "Dawn, how long have you been here?"

He furrowed his eyebrow. "In the Sanctuary?" She nodded. "I arrived shortly after Justice, so it has been ten years. My parents thought it would be a great honor for the family if I was accepted. They own a small farm in the countryside of Vanaheim. It is a big deal for someone in a poor family to be chosen to become Einherja."

A slow smile spread across her face. "I bet your parents are very proud of you. Thank you so much for helping me."

Dawn nodded. "You did a good job; we can practice tomorrow, if you would like. You should rest a bit." Serena thanked him again as he left the room. Looking around for the tabby cat, she found Marbles fast asleep near the climbing ropes. *What a life.*

She looked up at the ropes and took a deep breath. "Let's do this. This time, let's not fall down." She wrapped her hands around the rope, pulling her body onto the net. When she reached the middle, both arms began to wobble and her hands slipped off.

"Ouch!" She landed right on her butt on the cushioned floor. *Thankfully, there is something to break my fall: my big, squishy butt.* Laughing, Serena pulled herself off the mat and shook her arms out. "Well, that didn't go as planned. Let's do it again."

Marbles looked up at her with his sleepy blue eyes, letting

out the laziest meow. Serena nodded. "Don't worry about me —I'm good, Marbles." Wrapping her hands round the rope, she pulled her body up. Each movement made her arms tremble. Once again reaching the middle, Serena fell off. "Aargh!" Serena yelled with all her might as drops of sweat rolled down her cheek. "I need to do this!" After another several attempts, she swore her arms were about to fall off. "One last time." She grunted loudly as she pulled her heavy body past the middle, finally reaching the top.

Serena danced around the room, wincing while she waved both sore arms. "Finally, Serena Super Bad Ass Barista made it to the top."

Exhausted, she returned to her room, placing Marbles down on the mattress. Unbuckling the belt, she slipped the sheaths and daggers underneath the bed. Her entire body ached down to her bones. Serena shuffled like a zombie to the bathroom, each step ricocheting pain through her arms. After throwing her clothes into the hamper next to the door, she turned the metal taps on hot to fill the bath. Serena slowly slipped her body down into the soothing hot water. *Ah! I wonder where Erik is. I haven't seen him all day.*

After the relaxing bath, she braided her wet hair and slipped on a pair of leggings and a baggy sweater. Walking past Aimee's room, she placed her ear against the door but couldn't hear anything from within.

Discreetly, she opened the door. Aimee was still asleep on the bed, next to Justice. Backtracking down the hall, she went up to Erik's door and knocked.

"Erik? Are you in your room? Do you need anything?" There was no response. Her stomach growled, reminding her that she hadn't eaten since yesterday.

She made her way down to the dining room. Dawn, Aidan and Gamble sat around the table, telling each other stories about Justice. Dawn threw his head back and roared with laughter.

"Remember that one time when Justice was fighting that winged Ifrit? He completely forgot that weapons wouldn't even make a scratch on them. It burnt off one of his eyebrows and half of his head of hair. He was so embarrassed he wouldn't leave his room for three weeks." All three of the boys laughed and dug into their spaghetti-filled plates.

Serena surveyed the room for a moment before she turned to the boys. "Have you guys seen Erik today?" Dawn and Gamble shook their heads and went back to eating.

Aidan looked up at Serena. "Sorry, Serena. I tried to find him earlier, but he wasn't in his office or his room. None of us are sure exactly where he went."

She bit down on her lip. "Thank you."

A loud *slap* sounded from outside the Sanctuary. Aidan jumped off the chair, whipping around. "What was that?" No one answered. The ground began to ripple and the walls shook, causing some of the plates to fall off the table and pictures to the ground. Serena grabbed onto whatever she could reach, while the boys grabbed hold of their plates. As the tremors slowly died down, Dawn stood up.

"Everyone good? It's spring time. You know we get a couple of earthquakes every year."

Serena pushed the plates back from the edge of the table. "This one seemed a little stronger than the usual ones."

Dawn shrugged, walking towards the kitchen. He opened the door and popped his head inside. "Is everything okay after that quake?"

Nathaniel came out of the kitchen. "No need to worry yourselves. Everything is fine."

Aidan and Gamble grabbed their dirty plates, handing them to him. "Great supper, Nathaniel." Nathaniel nodded, heading back into the kitchen with the dirty dishes. The boys left the dining room and Serena scooped some spaghetti and meatballs onto her plate. Nathaniel came out of the kitchen, carrying a wet dishcloth, and began to wipe down the wooden table.

"Nathaniel, have you seen Erik today?"

He shook his head as he finished the cleaning. "Sorry, Miss Serena. I haven't seen him since yesterday."

She nervously tapped her fingers on top of the table. *It seems like I am the only one worried that Erik is nowhere to be found.* Serena grabbed the rest of the dishes and brought them back into the kitchen.

She headed towards Erik's office. Standing in the hallway, she knocked lightly on his door. "Erik? Are you in there?" Again, there was no answer. *I guess he still needs some space.* Walking back through the dining room into the library, she stopped to look at the bookshelf closest to the stairs. Blowing the dust from off the books, Serena let out a giant sneeze. She rubbed her nose and pulled out a golden rimmed book: *Baldr: The God loved by all.* Yawning as she walked back to her room, she curled up on top of the bed and opened the book.

"Baldr was the second son of Odin and Frigg. Unlike Thor with his mighty hammer and strength, Baldr was revered for his beauty and grace. His tragic death and betrayal of Loki led to the events of the battle of Ragnarok." Closing the book, she laid her head down on the soft pillow and fell asleep.

# CHAPTER SIX

A WEEK PASSED BY. JUSTICE NEVER WOKE UP, AND AIMEE, UNDER no circumstances, left the room. After training with Dawn, every day Serena would sit patiently and wait by Erik's door. As the days passed, Dawn finally informed her that Erik would often disappear for a week or two at a time—though he had once instructed Dawn to write updates on a piece of paper and leave it in front of the archway portal. Serena clicked her tongue in annoyance.

Shuffling through the night stand, she pulled out a notepad and pen.

*Erik, please come back. I need to know you're okay.*

*— Serena.*

She rushed into the attic, placing the note on the base of the metal archway.

Serena whirled back down the stairs and made her way to her bedroom. A black digital clock sat in front of her door with a yellow sticky note on top. Picking up the clock, she read the note.

*Miss Serena, here is the clock you requested.*

*— Nathaniel.*

She plugged in the clock and placed it on the nightstand

before turning the dial on the radio to find Avonmore's one and only radio station.

*"In other news, the manager of the local coffee shop, the Steaming Mugs, was found murdered last night around one am. Police are looking for any witnesses and are advising locals to stay indoors after ten pm, as this is the third homicide within a month. No news yet as to when the coffee shop will reopen."*

A wave of sorrow made its way up through her body, making her head begin to throb. Serena lay down on the bed, pulling the blanket over her head. She slammed down on the radio. Warm tears rolled down her cheeks, sticking the stray hairs to her face. Letting out a deep breath, she pushed the hair off her face. Her body shook and a twinge of pain flickered in her heart. She kicked off the blanket in a fit. "Why would anyone kill him? I just can't stay here and sit on my ass."

Serena kneeled on the ground and pulled out her sheath, tightly buckling it around her waist. She pulled Erik's grey sweatshirt over it. She creaked the door open and peeked down the hall.

*The coast is clear.* Serena quietly tip-toed down the stairs, carefully checking each room before she entered. She finally reached the front and snuck out the door.

In the middle of the rocky driveway stood a golden water fountain in the shape of a horn. The sound of the bubbling water spurting from it soothed her shaky nerves. On the far left stood a stand-alone garage that parked a black Toyota Corolla and a couple of muddy dirt bikes. The edge of the rocky road was overgrown with pink, purple and blue flowers, and the intense smell of lavender filled the air. As the sun began to set, Serena found herself amongst the slouchy weeping willow trees surrounding the property.

She followed the dirt road until the willow trees became pine trees and she arrived at the highway. Both legs grew tired as she trudged down the road that took her to the outskirts of Avonmore. She crept through a backyard, ducking underneath the patio to avoid being noticed by the family sitting watching a movie. Opening the fence gate, she ran across the lawn and into another empty backyard. As she tried to wiggle the next gate open, a loud creak filled the quiet night. Her eyes grew big and she shook her head. *You're going to wake someone up.* Gripping the rough edges of the wood, Serena hoisted herself up and over the fence. Letting out relieved sigh, she landed softly on the ground. *Cat woman has nothing on me! Whew!* She wiped the sweat rolling off her forehead. More yards were crossed until Serena reached the main street. The Avonmore pub light sputtered, followed by a hum, loud music, and chattering from inside.

The police had barricade tape blocking the front door of the Steaming Mugs. Serena ducked underneath the tape and tried to turn the doorknob, rolling her eyes at her belief that it may have been unlocked. Annoyed with herself, she made her way up the main street.

A light thudding came from behind her.

She whipped around, but nobody was there.

An eerie wave of cold air went through Serena, down to her bones. Her body rippled from the chill, sending goosebumps down her spine.

Nothing was behind her, but she ran the rest of the way to her house. She scurried through the door and locked it. One knee after the other, Serena crawled on the floor to the front window and slowly pulled back the curtains, looking outside. *You are being paranoid. Chill out, Serena.* Whatever she thought was behind her refused to pop out of the darkness, even after ten minutes. Each knee throbbed when she arose from the hardwood floor.

She flipped the light switches to get out of the darkness and opened the wooden closet in the front entry. Digging through the empty boxes and winter clothing, she pulled out a purple backpack. She grabbed her family photo album from the rickety book shelf propped against the wall. Gently placing it in her backpack, she glanced around the room to see if there was anything else she wanted to take. Few photos hung on the walls, but she pulled a couple off, placing them in the photo album.

She headed straight into the bathroom, opened the door to the vanity, and pulled out her hair straighteners, along with her favorite shampoo and conditioner. Twisting the lid off the shampoo, she sniffed the top. *Oh coconut, my hair has missed your mystical detangling powers.* Laughing to herself, she put the shampoo bottle into a plastic bag before she placed it in the backpack.

Everything else was in her room. Opening the dresser, she pulled out as many clothes as she could fit and shoved them into the bag, letting out exasperated grunt while doing so. A puff of air came out of the backpack as she struggled to zip it up. "Whew!"

A noise came from downstairs.

Quickly, she looked through the bedroom window. A dark figure stood in front of the door. Whoever they were, they raised their leg up, slamming it down into the door. After a few minutes of silence, the high-pitched shatter of glass came from the living room, and the hardwood boards let out a moaning creak.

Heavy footsteps came stomping up the stairs.

Serena pulled out both of her daggers and hid behind the bedroom door. The footsteps stopped for a minute as the bathroom door creaked. Then, they continued down the hall. As the steps came closer, the smell of rotting flesh filled Serena's nose, making her stomach queasy.

The intruder strolled into the room, dressed in a robe. He bent down, looking underneath the bed, before drifting towards the closet and pulling open the wooden doors.

Serena jumped out from behind the door and rushed towards the robed man. Slamming her body into his back, the man toppled to the ground. Without any pause, he rolled around and kicked Serena square in the stomach with such force that she was flung across the room into the wall. The intruder jumped back on to his feet and lunged towards her. As he did, the robe shifted, revealing the man's face. He matched the attackers in her dreams. The flesh around his mouth was discolored, hanging only by a thread of skin. Where the eyes should have been were two empty sockets. Serena could swear she saw something crawling in the darkness of them.

It wrapped an abnormally cool hand around her throat and slammed her into the wall again. Serena clawed at the hand as she felt her breath become jagged and blocked. He raised her up to eye level. "The Goddess will be pleased," his deep voice chuckled, sending chills down her spine. Her eyes became unfocused as the small breath struggled to release. Her voice was strained.

"Think again, idiot." She lifted both daggers and inserted them deep underneath his ear lobes.

She pulled them until they met in the middle of his throat. Black blood sprayed from the wound, drenching her face. His head flopped over as the limp body fell to the ground, finally freeing Serena's throat. A strong sulphuric smell erupted as he liquefied into a big black puddle.

Serena wheezed for air and fell to her knees. Her stomach turned from the overwhelming smell. Trying to avoid the puddle, she vomited all over the floor.

One foot at a time, she shuffled into the bathroom and turned the tub taps as hot as her skin could handle. As the bathtub filled, she grabbed some towels from the closet and headed back into her room to wipe down the puddle of goo and vomit. "You couldn't just turn into a pile of dust like in *Buffy*. Nope. You just had to turn into messy goo." Serena sauntered downstairs, shoving the soiled towels into a garbage bag. Her stomach growled. The moment she opened the fridge, a bottle of rosé screamed her name. She grabbed the bottle and crumpled a garbage bag into her pocket.

"Sorry, stomach. I think need this more than I need food."

As Serena walked back up to the bathroom, she twisted the top off the bottle and took a huge swig. Turning off the tap, she pulled off her filthy clothes and shoved them into the garbage bag.

Serena stared in the mirror, outlining the fresh red and blue bruises along her neck. Grabbing the bottle of wine, she slowly lowered herself into the hot bath. "What have I got myself into?" She finished off the bottle, placed the empty on the ledge and unplugged the bath with her toe.

Her feet blurred as she staggered back to the bedroom, stopping often to lean against the wall. The smell of vomit and rotten eggs lingered in the room and her head began to spin. Both hands reached out to find a wall or anything to hold her up. The spinning went faster. At this point, she could barely stand up, so Serena laid her head down on the cool hardwood and fell asleep.

When she opened her eyes, she stood in the middle of Avonmore Park. The robed creature, his head held on by a thread, manifested out of thin air as if he were a spirit. "Where there is one, there will be many more. The ritual will continue. The blood of a god will spill." He glided towards her, continuing to repeat, "Where there is one, there will be many more." His voice cracked as blood gurgled out of his nearly headless neck.

The earth began to tremor, and the ground cracked around Serena. Hundreds of the robed creatures climbed out of the broken ground, surrounding her. Dozens of hands grabbed her body, pulling her down on to the ground. "Daughter of Nótt, your sacrifice will not be in vain."

She shrieked.

Waking up on the hardwood floor, her body shivered from a cold sweat. Her temples pounded as if she were in the middle of a drum circle. She yanked her body up, dragged herself to the closet and pulled out a pair of dark jeans and a t-shirt. She grabbed a comb off her dresser and quickly pulled it through her kinky hair, then slowly lugged herself down into the kitchen. The first thing Serena did was brew a fresh pot of coffee. *"Where there is one, there will be many more.* They know where I live. This has to be the last time I come here."

The coffee machine flashed and beeped piercingly. "Finally." She scooped sugar into her mug as she took in the warm aroma of the hot coffee. Her shoulders began to relax, and the throbbing in her head came to a halt while she considered what to do with the house.

Serena grabbed the thick yellow phone book off the top of the fridge. She slammed it down on the table and flipped through the pages to look for a number for a moving company, finally hiring one from Langley to pack away the house and put all her belongings into a prepaid storage unit. Nearly drinking the whole pot of coffee, she looked up the number of the only real estate agent in Avonmore. "Yes, Martha. I will leave the keys under the front steps, and on the kitchen counter I will leave all my contact information. Thank you for understanding the urgency of my situation and for hiring a company to clean my house." Dumping the rest of the coffee down the drain, she washed her dirty dishes.

Serena found another bag in the front entry closet and checked over the house one last time, filling it with more of her belongings before booking a taxi. She hung up her cellphone and ran upstairs to grab her backpack. Locking her house for the last time, she hid the keys underneath the front steps. "It's time to let go."

The taxi came speeding down Main Street and parked adjacent from the house. A single tear rolled down her face and she took a deep breath while giving the house one last glance. "If you can hear me, Mom and Dad, I'm sorry for leaving." Serena grabbed the bags and tried to hold back her tears as she walked closer to the taxi.

The taxi driver stared at Serena's freshly bruised neck as he loaded his trunk with the bags.

"Miss, do you need to go to the hospital?" She gave him a weak smile and shook her head.

"Oh no. I'm just very clumsy and fell down the stairs." Neither said a single word until they reached the highway. The driver was confused when she told him to drop her off on the side of it, next to the Langley sign. He slowed down the taxi and came to a halt.

"Miss, there's nothing around here but trees and animals. Are you sure you'll be okay?" Serena nodded as she opened the car door.

"Yes, thank you for your concern. I'll be fine; I'm perfectly capable of taking care of myself." She handed him a twenty-dollar bill. He grabbed the bags from the trunk and placed them down on the road. He drove away slowly, every so often looking back at her. Serena gave him a quick wave goodbye.

Looking up at tops of the trees, she found the one flashing pine tree which towered above all others. She walked through the trees, reaching the dirt road, and followed the weeping willows to the edge of the wild flowers. "*Oppstå.*" Serena let out a relieved sigh as the Sanctuary appeared in front of her, thankful she hadn't forgotten the word.

Erik rushed out of the door and brushed his fingers across Serena's bruise. "What the hell happened to your neck? Where have you been?"

Frowning, Serena pushed his hands off.

"Where have *I* been? You must be kidding. You've been gone for a whole week. Where have *you* been?" She felt her cheeks burn as the anger boiled through her body. "You can't just tell me that you like me and leave for an entire week without saying a single word. After what happened with your father, you didn't care if I was okay or if Justice was still alive. You don't..."

His face turned red and his usually calm eyes were enraged. "You don't know what I have been through and how close I was to killing my father. You don't know me."

Avoiding his gaze, she quickly went around him into the door. "You're right, Erik; I really don't know you."

She stomped her feet all the way to her room and threw her bags down on the ground. Her backpack burst open and the clothes scattered all around the floor. Serena exhaled loudly and shook her head. *He could have told me he needed space, or at least let me know he was okay.* She sat on the ground, picking up scattered clothes. Hanging half of them in her closet, she folded the rest and left them on the closet floor. Reaching the bottom of her bag, she pulled out the picture frames and placed them on top of her nightstand, noting that she needed to ask Nathaniel for some nails and a hammer to hang them up.

Outlining her parents' faces with her finger, Serena's eyes began to swell with tears. "God, I miss you guys so much. I wonder if you knew about Nótt? I can only imagine what you would think about this!"

Grabbing her family photo album from the backpack, she lay down on top of the bed. Flipping through the pages, she reminisced about all the fun she had with them. The photo album began with a picture of her mother with long, curly brown hair, covered with fresh flowers, standing in front of their house in Avonmore. Her father, with shaggy brown hair and bright blue eyes, had his arms wrapped around her mother's pregnant belly.

Unpacked boxes were scattered across the lawn and covered the front entry stairs. "Where did they live before Avonmore?" Serena rubbed her chin as she tried to recall if they'd ever told her. Flipping the page, the next picture was of her parents cradling newborn Serena on top their bed. "Oh,

Mom. You couldn't make it fast enough to the hospital. Luckily Mormor was around to deliver me." She let out a small chuckle. "You were such a strong woman; I would have definitely panicked."

Flipping further into the photo album, the next picture was of Serena, no older than four, with long, curly hair, sitting on a pile of wrapping paper. Her face was smeared with chocolate cake and she had the goofiest grin. Next to Serena was her mother and her Mormor, who could have passed for her mother's older sister.

At the end of the photo album was a picture of Serena at six years old, wearing a velvet black dress while she held a dozen red roses. That day, her mother and father had sat her down at the kitchen table to tell her that Mormor had passed away. Her father took this picture before they went to the graveyard to say goodbye.

She felt lucky she'd had sixteen wonderful years with her parents.

Serena let out a big yawn and her heavy eyes began to close. She laid her head down on top of the photo album. As she fell asleep, she wondered what Erik's childhood had been like.

ફ્જ

A small boy no older than five was huddled in a dark corner of a kitchen, whimpering as he wrapped his arms tightly against his knees. Serena slid down against the wall beside the boy. She lifted his chin up and wiped away his tears. "Are you okay? Where's your mother?"

The boy wiped his running nose on his sleeve. "You shouldn't be here. He is coming."

Henrik came storming into the kitchen, knocking over the wooden table. "You need to learn your place, boy. We do not speak of the filthy blood running through your mother's veins. If you ever tell anyone about her again, it will be the last thing you do." Henrik grabbed a fistful of the boy's shirt. Serena tried to grab Henrik's arm, but her hand fell through it. A young woman with long brown hair and violet eyes came running into the kitchen, carry a newborn baby.

"Henrik, please, it was a mistake. He will never do it again. Right, Erik?" Erik lowered his face and nodded slowly. Henrik pushed him against the wall and stormed out of the room. Ailsa knelt in front of Erik, gently rubbing the side of his cheek. "One day, my beautiful son, I will help you and your brother escape. Your father is frightened over the powerful blood coursing through your veins. You both have a destiny that will shake up this world. You, Erik Baldr, are blessed by Odin."

Turning towards Serena, Ailsa smiled. "Serena, you have a major role to play in his destiny. Never give up on him. Promise me you always will help my son." Serena's mouth dropped as she slowly nodded her head.

Serena gasped as she quickly sat up. "He said he wanted to kill his father. Henrik was the reason Ailsa killed herself. She knew when Erik left that Justice would become the next punching bag. She must have known if she died, Henrik would send Justice away. She protected her sons by sacrificing herself." She slammed her hand into her face. "How could I be so *stupid*?" Serena yelled at herself, wiping the tears from her cheeks.

Darting off the bed, she ran across to Erik's door, banging as hard as she could. "Please, Erik. I need you to open the door."

Erik opened the door with tousled hair and half-asleep eyes. He let out a big yawn. "Serena, what are you doing? Its three am." She pushed him further into the room, kicking the door shut behind her.

"I'm sorry for barging into your room. I'm also sorry I've been so stupid. You're right, I don't know what you've been through, and I want to be here for you." Her heart pounded so hard, she thought it might fly out of her chest.

Erik nodded as he wrapped his arms around her shoulders. "I am sorry, too. I shouldn't have left you or Justice. I just needed space to think and process." Serena kissed Erik's soft chin, while he traced his fingers down her cheek. "I almost forgot how beautiful you are."

Serena laughed. "You're such a smooth talker. I'm sure you say that to all the girls who come barging into your room in the middle of the night...especially the ones with smeared makeup down their faces."

He picked her up and threw her down on top of his bed. "Nope. Just you." Laughing, Serena rolled her eyes.

"Sure."

Erik nodded, laying down next to her. He pulled the thick brown blanket over them.

"Now go to sleep, and we can talk tomorrow."

Serena kissed his cheek. "I wish we could just stay in your room forever."

Erik mumbled, "Then who would bring you coffee and make me delicious cookies?" She wrapped her arms around his back.

"That is so true. I just want to hide from the world and be safe with you."

He began to snore loudly, and she kissed his back.

"I made a promise to your mom, and I intend to keep it."

# CHAPTER SEVEN

WHEN SERENA AWOKE, ERIK SAT SHIRTLESS ON THE WINDOW SILL. *Now, that is a perfect sight to wake up to.* The crack in the window blew a cool breeze, and goosebumps rose up on her arms. Serena grabbed Erik's shirt off the floor and slipped it on.

"Good morning, Erik." Serena came up behind him and wrapped her arms around his warm back. He turned around, pulling her down onto his lap, and softly kissed her lips. "Good morning, Serena. You're absolutely glowing." Underneath her eyes felt sticky, the clumps of mascara blurring her vision slightly.

"I doubt my face is glowing; it's probably because I didn't wash off my makeup. I'm sorry for ruining your beauty sleep."

He lifted her chin and kissed her cheek. "You have a very hard time with compliments, don't you?" Erik was not wrong.

"I'm not like you. I'm not used to people saying nice things about me—I'm used to being alone." Erik tilted his head towards her.

"Well, you'd better get used to it, because you are great,

and I wish you saw what I see when I look at you." Erik cleared his throat. "The first time I met you, I felt like I already knew you from somewhere."

Serena's heart began to race. *Could it be real that I spoke to five-year-old Erik when I was dreaming?* She smiled. "Do you know what people say about déjà vu?" Erik shook his head. "My mother always said if you experience déjà vu, it means your life is on the right path."

Erik nodded. "That makes sense. I like that—my path is definitely leading to you. I won't go any other way."

She ran her fingers through his hair. "You're a little goofy."

Erik lifted Serena up onto the window sill. He changed into a short sleeved grey shirt with dark blue jeans. "I have some work I need to do in my office downstairs. You can stay in here as long as you want to. See you later?" He kissed the top of her head.

"Of course." As he left, she jumped into the shower. Serena grabbed the bar of soap and scrubbed her entire body. "Hah. This is how he always smells like cinnamon." Several minutes of pure bliss later, she stepped out of the shower. Serena wiped the steam off the mirror, running the comb through her hair. "Erik is right. For once, my skin looks pretty decent. It must be all the love in the air." Serena shook her head. "Erik's cheesiness is rubbing off on me." She scrunched her hair while walking into his closet. Sifting through the clothes, Serena settled on an oversized blue t-shirt. Her body was quite sore still, so she decided to just hang around Erik's room. She threw his dirty clothes into the hamper. "You know you spend too much time alone when you start having full conversations with yourself." Of all the bad habits she could have, talking to herself seemed to be the least damaging. After a few minutes of pacing through Erik's room, she noticed a glossy corner stuck out underneath a mountain of socks. Serena lifted the socks up and threw them into the hamper, revealing a picture lying on the ground. Five-year-old Erik sat on top of Ailsa's right knee, as she held baby Justice tightly in her arms. "She was so beautiful and so happy just holding her boys." Serena whispered a vow to Ailsa—a vow that promised to protect Erik from his father.

She placed the picture on top of the nightstand. "Erik?" Light knocking came from the door. "Have you seen Serena?" Serena walked towards the door, opened it a crack, and peeped her head through. Aimee's mouth dropped as she looked Serena up and down.

"SERENA! Why are you in Erik's room? You don't have pants on, and your hair is soaking wet!" Aimee giggled, pushing her way into the room. Serena knew her face was blushing. She tried to look as innocent as possible. "I've missed a lot, haven't I?" Aimee grinned. "I've been a terrible friend! When did this happen? Tell me EVERYTHING!" She nudged her pointy elbow into Serena's side. "Come on, spill it, Serena."

Serena nodded. "Okay, I will. Just relax, Aimee." Serena told her what had happened and just as she was about to finish Aimee squealed loudly, causing a ripple of ringing in Serena's ears. "I see we both have wicked taste in men."

Serena picked up her jeans off the floor and pulled them back on. "So, why were you looking for me?" Aimee twirled her blonde hair around her finger.

"I have a favor to ask you. Will you please come with me to Avonmore?"

"Of course, but why do you need to go?" Serena raised her eyebrows. *I didn't think she would leave the Sanctuary until Justice woke up.* Aimee nervously played with her fingers as she looked up at Serena.

"Please, promise me that you won't say anything to anyone—especially Erik. I'm not ready for anyone to know just yet."

Serena nodded. "Sure, I won't say anything." Aimee took a deep breath and shook out her hands.

"Okay, here goes. I'm a week late. I need to get a couple of pregnancy tests. I threw up a couple of days ago, and I just feel so tired all the time. I need to just get this over with." Serena shrieked, giving her friend a hug.

"That's great news! Justice is going to be so happy when he wakes up!" She went back to her room and slipped on a long tunic and black leggings with flats. She grabbed her sheath belt from underneath her bed and securely wrapped it around her waist, before writing Erik a quick note in case he tried to look for her.

*Erik, I am taking Aimee to Avonmore. I will have my cell phone if you need me. — Serena.*

The two girls met on the dirt road in front of the Sanctuary. "Thank you so much for coming with me, Serena. I really did not want to go alone."

Serena rubbed her hand against Aimee's arm. "It's not a problem. You're one of my only friends; I want to help you as much as I can. And who knows? Maybe one day, we will be sisters-in-law." Serena winked at Aimee.

"I sure hope so. It would be great to have a sister." Both girls giggled as they kept walking past the weeping willow trees. "You seem perkier than usual."

Aimee's face softened and she gave her friend a slight smile. "Last night I had a dream; it felt so real. I could feel Justice's arms wrapped around me and he told me to get out of my room. So here I am...plus, I really didn't want to ask Erik to get me a test. Talk about awkward!" After a few minutes, they reached the highway.

Serena turned towards Aimee, looking her friend up and down. "I don't want this to sound rude, but Aimee... everyone will notice you. How will hide your orange skin and your ears?"

"Oh, I guess you haven't been learning much about magic.

I thought Gamble and Aidan would have taken over the magic lessons—at least taught you the basic principles." Not a single person had even suggested learning magic to Serena; in fact, no one even brought up magic near her.

"I really don't see them often—usually only when they're eating. Dawn has been just focusing on training me to fight."

Aimee's lips tightened, letting out a sigh. "I will need to talk to them. You should know at least the basic spells. The elves created a very powerful glamour spell. It's hard to see, even to a magically trained eye. I will look the same to you, but to everyone else, I will just look like an ordinary eighteen-year-old girl." Aimee waved a hand above her and whispered. "*Doltha.*"

The girls continued down the highway until they reached one of Avonmore's cul de sacs. Walking through the small neighborhood, Aimee looked around at the houses. "Did you live somewhere close to here?"

Serena shook her head. "No, I lived on the other side of Avonmore." It seemed like Aimee was studying the neighbourhood. She let out a soft sigh.

"Sometimes, I fantasize about living in the non-magical world...having a white picket fence and working at a clothing store. I wonder, if Justice and I ran away, what our life would be like."

Serena shrugged. "I think it would be hard, ignoring all the magic and living a mundane life. Plus, if you ran away, I wouldn't get to hang out with you."

Aimee smiled. "I know, you're right. It would be hard for me to ignore the magic running through my veins. Magic will always be a part of me. Do you miss your life from before?"

Serena crinkled her nose. "No, not really. I wish I knew about magic and my abilities a long time ago. Maybe I could have saved my parents."

They walked past the small theatre. Serena pointed towards the Steaming Mugs café. "That's where I've worked for the past two years. It had great coffee, and delicious cookies." The building was dark and the yellow barricade tape still surrounded the door. Aimee went towards the bay window, sticking her face against the glass.

"What happened in there? It looks like someone went on a rampage—like a bull in a china shop."

Serena frowned, sticking her face against the glass. "My manager was found murdered there a couple of nights ago. I need to grab something important before we go back." Aimee nodded. Continuing their stroll, some locals passing by stopped Serena to tell her how sorry they were about Jeremy.

The girls reached the market, and both grabbed shopping baskets. Aimee followed Serena towards the pharmacy. For a few minutes, she stood in front of the pregnancy tests, finally grabbing a couple of boxes. "So, which one do I pick?"

Serena shrugged "Honestly, I have no idea. I'm sure it doesn't matter."

Aimee threw the boxes down into her basket. "Let's get some snacks." Walking into the snack aisle, they loaded up with chocolate and chips. As they walked towards the cashier, Serena noticed a row of picture frames against the wall.

"Hold on a minute, Aimee. I'd like to pick out a frame for Erik." She grabbed a shiny silver one. They placed the items on top of the conveyor belt.

"Hey, Serena, how are you doing?" the older cashier asked.

"Oh hey, Frank, I'm doing well." Frank rang through the items, giving Serena a sly look.

"I didn't know you were seeing anyone." She laughed and put her hands up.

"It's not for me, Frank. It's for my cousin Aimee, from Langley." Aimee blushed and Frank laughed.

"Well, you girls stay out of trouble."

Serena paid the bill. "Thanks, Frank."

When they walked out the door, Aimee's stomach

growled. "I am so hungry; let's go eat some food." Serena's stomach grumbled at the mere mention of it.

"Sure, let's go to the pub. That's pretty much the only place around here."

Backtracking down Main Street, they arrived at Avonmore's pub. It had been one of the oldest buildings in the small town—anyone with two eyes could see it, from the decaying pale bricks to the chipped wooden door. A couple of older men sat on the bench outside the pub smoking. Serena never asked their names before, but all she knew was that they had sat in that same spot for the past eighteen years.

The girls went into the pub and sat in a booth next to the multi-colored stained window. The pub wasn't busy; a group of elderly women sat behind the girls' stall, and a couple of patrons sat at the bar. A peppy red-headed waitress approached their table.

"Hey Serena, I haven't seen you around for a while. It is so scary, what happened to Jeremy—and I saw a sign on your front lawn that you're selling your house!" The waitress handed the girls two menus. As Serena opened her menu, she looked up at the waitress.

"Yes, Poppy. After the incident at the Steaming Mugs, I'm moving to Langley with my cousin Aimee." Poppy looked confused.

"Oh, I didn't think you had any family."

Aimee grinned. "Second cousins."

Poppy's eyebrow raised as she nodded her head. "All right, ladies, what can I get for you today?" Aimee ordered a burger with fries and a large chocolate milkshake. Serena ordered a small Hawaiian pizza with hot pepper and a glass of water. In no time at all, Poppy brought them their drinks. "Thanks, Poppy." Serena gave the waitress the sweetest smile.

The elderly women behind Aimee gossiped loudly. Serena watched them closely. She knew this was the best way to catch up on the town's latest news. The one with short curly hair whispered to the others.

"This afternoon, when I was filling out a report at the police station, I overheard the sheriff talking to his deputy. He said Mariah's body was found on top of a pentagram. The bottom half of her body looked like it had been eaten. And I guess the poor manager of the Steaming Mugs was also found on top of a pentagram."

The two other women gasped. "Strange things are happening in our small town. The murders and the two earthquakes within a week or so of each other."

All the women agreed. "Strange things indeed."

Aimee lowered her head and whispered. "Serena, did you know about the pentagrams?"

Serena tapped her fingers against the table. "No. Now we really can't go back to the Sanctuary without investigating the café."

Aimee shook her head. "I really don't know about this."

Serena waved her hand down. "Oh, don't worry, it'll be fine. We will be in and out and back to the Sanctuary in no time."

Poppy sat their food down on the table. Aimee dug into her fries. "Thanks Poppy, I'm starving." Poppy giggled and twirled around, heading back towards the bar.

"Enjoy your food, and let me know if you need anything else."

"This is so good. I feel like I could eat about ten orders of fries," Aimee said, stuffing her face. Serena laughed, biting down on a slice of pizza. Aimee finished off her burger and fries, before staring at the leftover pizza on top of the table.

"Serena, are you going to finish your pizza?" She shook her head and passed the pizza across the table. "You are a good friend."

Aimee finished off the pizza and washed it down with her milkshake. "Do you feel better?" Aimee's face dropped, and she shook her head. "Uh…which way is the bathroom?" Serena pointed to the door next to the bar.

Aimee covered her mouth and ran towards the bathroom. Poppy came back to the table.

"Is she going to be okay? Was there something wrong with the food?"

Serena shook her head. "No, everything was great. I think she ate too much food; I'll be right back."

Serena picked up her glass of water and took the bags into the bathroom. When she walked through the door, Aimee had just flushed the toilet. She shuffled out the stall, washed her hands and splashed some cool water on her face. "I feel better now."

"You really should take these tests." Serena handed her the plastic bag.

"You're right; let's just get this over with." Aimee went back into the stall and took all four of the tests. Serena sat on top of the counter, tapping her fingers patiently. "Well, here it goes." Aimee placed the tests on the counter. They both waited in silence.

A positive sign appeared underneath the little plastic window on the first test.

A couple minutes later, all the tests had positive signs.

"I just knew it! There is no way a normal person eats this much food." Aimee hugged Serena as a couple of tears rolled down her cheeks. "I can't wait until Justice wakes up; he will be so happy. He always talked about starting a family one day."

Serena wiped the tears off her cheeks. "You two will be great parents."

Aimee's stomach rumbled. "Oh no! I think I'm hungry again."

The girls laughed as they looped their arms together. "Well, I could use a coffee; let's go get you a snack."

As they sat back down, the other customers had already

left. Poppy came towards their booth. "Well, ladies, would you like anything else? We'll be closing soon, but I can get something for you to take away if you'd like?" The girls nodded. Serena ordered a large coffee, and Aimee ordered a slice of apple pie.

The girls sat on the bench in front of the pub while Poppy and the cook locked up. "Hey, girls, you need to get going soon. The police have pushed back the town curfew to nine pm. Will you be okay to get to wherever you're staying?"

Serena nodded. "Yes, we'll be fine. Please stay safe." Poppy sighed and started walking up the street with the cook, before turning towards the girls. She said, "The same to the both of you. Be careful; there's something evil out there." The girls watched the pair walk up the main street, disappearing into the distance.

"Serena, I really think we should be heading back to the Sanctuary."

Serena shook her head. "Not yet. I need to go into the café and see if I can find any clues about Jeremy's murder."

Aimee frowned. "Maybe we should call the others?"

Serena stood up and looked around to see if anyone was near. "No, it will be okay. Like I said before, we'll be in and out before anyone even notices we are gone."

She ducked underneath the barricade tape and took out her keys, and lifted the tape so Aimee could duck underneath. Broken cups and coffee beans were scattered across the ground. The chairs and tables were flipped over. On the middle of the floor, someone had drawn a black pentagram. Crusty blood was splattered around it. Serena took a deep breath.

"Poor Jeremy. I should have been here to protect him."

Aimee shook her head. "Serena, I am sorry about your friend. But it's lucky you weren't here—this could have been you."

As she looked at the pentagram, a memory flashed in her

mind—Serena being held down on a similar pentagram as the robed men carved into her skin. She covered her mouth with her hand, lightly tapping her lips. "Aimee, I think I know what did this. Well, I'm not sure exactly what they are, but I am certain that I know *who* did this. Why couldn't I have connected the dots before?"

"What are you talking about? How would you know?" Aimee frowned.

Serena couldn't take her eyes off the pentagram. "I had this reoccurring dream for the past two years of these robed men sacrificing me on a similar pentagram. The other day, I snuck out of the Sanctuary to investigate Jeremy's death. I had to go back to my house to grab my keys. One of the robed men followed me home and attacked me. I killed him." Serena paced around the pentagram. "Well, they aren't quite men. Maybe creatures? No...zombies? I'm not sure exactly what they are."

"SERENA! Did you tell anyone about what happened? You could have been killed." Aimee grabbed Serena's arms.

"Well, I was going to tell someone, but Erik showed up and we fought. Then, we made up. I didn't want to ruin the moment we were having by bringing up what happened."

Aimee rolled her eyes, shaking her head slowly "Yeah, I know what happened next." Aimee sat down next to the front window. "This is not good, Serena. Your dreams, the pentagrams and robed creatures? What does it all mean?"

Serena took out her phone.

"I'm not sure what it all means, but I think those weird zombie/demon/rotten flesh face creatures, or whatever the hell they are, are responsible for Jeremy's and Mariah's deaths. I'd better take some pictures of the pentagram to show Erik." Serena looked down at her phone. "Twenty missed calls from an unknown number, and four new voicemails." She dialed her voicemail number. Erik's voice began talking "Serena, it's Erik. I need you to call me back right away. It's about Justice..."

Serena dialed the number, and Erik picked up the phone. "Hello? Serena? Is that you?"

Aimee jumped off her chair. "Serena, get down now! Someone is coming."

Without a thought, her body crumpled down on the ground. She fumbled to press the power button on the phone. Four robed men marched past the front window of the café, dragging a girl. The girl's body was so limp, it reminded Serena of a raggedy Ann doll.

Serena's phone rang.

*Shit.*

Two of the robed men came towards the café. "Aimee, hide and call Erik. I'll distract them." Aimee nodded, grabbed the cell phone, and hid behind the counter.

Serena took out her daggers and ran as fast as she could out of the café.

"Hey, freaks, are you looking for me?" The two robed men picked up the pace and ran towards her. She rushed towards the one on the right. Lifting her dagger, she slashed him the face before kicking him hard in the stomach. He groaned, falling to the ground. The other robed man came up behind Serena and grabbed her arms. He picked her straight up, slamming her against the pavement. She strained to jump back up and kicked as hard as she could, directly in the middle of his knee.

A sickening snap filled the air as he screamed, tumbling down.

She jabbed both of her daggers into his empty eye sockets, pulled them out, and whipped the daggers across his throat. Black blood bubbled out of the gash. Sulphur erupted out of his body as he liquefied into a black puddle.

The first robed man came up behind Serena, digging his sharp nails into her shoulders. He slammed himself against her, sending her crashing down into the ground, hitting her head against the road. Lifting his foot high in the air, he slammed it down onto her back. She twisted her arm back, stabbing him in the Achilles'. As blood gushed out of his heel, he staggered back and crumbled to the ground. She pulled her sore body back up and silt his throat. The robed man screamed like a banshee as he liquefied into a puddle.

A small ringing shot through Serena's head. She tried to shake it off, running up the street. "Where do I go?"

A blood curdling scream came from the direction of the church. *Shit. Come on, short legs. Let's go.*

She turned around and ran towards the church. Almost out of breath, she ran up the concrete steps, the ground beneath her starting to shake. A loud crackling made the tar on the road split open. Serena opened her arms to try to balance herself. She staggered back down the stairs, while the tremors slowly died off. Finally, she rushed through the wooden church doors. On the floor, the girl was flopped over in the middle of a pentagram, blood pooling out of her. *Too late.*

Around the pentagram, the four chanting robed men kneeled on the ground and lifted their hands in the air. "This offering is for the Goddess." The robed man in blue stood up, walking down the aisle towards Serena. "Daughter of Nótt, you are too late." Serena whipped back around and ran out the church.

*Was there a bad guy newsletter with my face on it? How do they all recognize me?* The robed men piled out of the church, following Serena. Without watching her step, her foot missed the edge and she fell, her ankle twisting awkwardly. *Get up!* Serena limped towards the road, heading for the Steaming Mugs.

She pushed her body as hard as she could, trying to pick up the pace, but was overcome by two of the robed men. As they wrapped their clammy hands around her arms, the prominent smell of dead flesh slithered up her nose. "Let go of me!" Mimicking a wave, she whipped both arms around, trying to gather some wiggle room.

"Little bitch." One attacker punched her in the stomach. *Oomph.* Serena's knees buckled from the force of the blow. She had the faintest taste of blood and bile in her mouth. Two cool hands dug into her cheeks, pulling her body to stand up without any effort. "I am going to enjoy carving up your soft, fleshy body." He let out a menacing chuckle.

With a flick of her neck, Serena pulled her head back and smashed her forehead directly into his face. The bone in his nose made a sickening crunch. He screamed and covered it as blood oozed out and fell backwards, yelling for the others to deal with her.

"I don't think so."

The two robed men shoved her down onto the ground. The brown robed man held her arms down, and the other in black held her legs. The robed man in blue pulled out long dagger from his waistband. "The goddess won't mind if I cut you up a bit before the ritual." He dragged the dagger across her cheek. Serena winced as blood droplets trickled down her skin. She bit down on her lip. "I want to hear you scream, daughter of the night."

Lowering the dagger, he slowly pushed it into her shoulder. Serena could feel it rub against her bone. "Scream for me, and I will stop."

Serena clenched her jaw. "Shut up!" He pushed the dagger in deeper, blood gushed out of her wound. Serena refused to scream; she wouldn't give them the satisfaction of winning.

*Take a deep breath. It will all be over soon.*

# CHAPTER EIGHT

AIMEE RAN DOWN THE STREET, LIFTED BOTH HER HANDS UP AND yelled, *"AMAR!"* A huge boulder materialized, crushing the robed attacker.

"Aimee, get out of here and RUN!" Serena shouted. Tires screeched down the street and a black Corolla came to a halt in front of the theatre. Erik jumped out of the car, followed immediately by Justice. He pulled out a long sword from the sheath wrapped around his back and rushed towards the robed men.

"Serena, are you okay?'

A wave of relief washed over Serena's body. "Yes. I'm glad you decided to finally make it."

Erik shook his head. "Even in the middle of a fight, you have time to be sarcastic."

Serena grinned. "Of course. Now, can you please kill these guys?"

The two robed men released Serena. "Enough of your senseless talking."

In unison, the men pulled out short swords from underneath their robes and ran towards Erik, circling around him one on either side. He spun, lifted his sword up, and hacked an arm off each of them.

He spun again; with one final whip of his sword, both men were decapitated.

The final robed man crawled on top of Serena, pulled out his dagger, and pressed it against her throat. "This one is mine!"

A bolt whooshed passed Serena's ear, landing directly in the robed man's skull and leaving a splatter of black blood over her face. *Bleh!* Justice lifted a metal crossbow up into the air like a trophy and yelled, "Bullseye!"

A small mushroom cloud of sulphur surrounded the Einherja as all the robed men liquefied. Erik scrunched his nose, turning away. Justice covered his mouth with the sleeve on his arm.

"That's new. I've never seen anyone turn into black goo before."

At speed, Aimee ran into Justice's arms. "I knew you were going to wake up. I missed you so much! I've been beside you the whole time." Her tears turned to laughter and Justice kissed them off her cheeks.

"I know, Aimee; your voice was the only thing that kept me fighting."

Aimee held onto his arm as tight as she could, making their way back to the car. Serena's head throbbed and her body ached as if she had been hit by a bus. She fought to keep her eyes open.

"Erik, you have good timing—though it would have been nice if you were maybe five minutes earlier."

"Oh, come on now. You should have just stayed on the phone."

*Why didn't I think of that?*

Erik rushed to Serena's side, bent down, and scooped her up into his arms.

"What were you thinking?" his voice growled as he

clenched both cheeks. She gently rubbed the side of his face, the scruff tickling her fingertips.

"Please don't be angry; I just wanted to help that girl. I didn't make it in time, and they killed her—but I killed two of those demons or zombie things, whatever the hell they are."

He smiled down at her, and placed a soft kiss on her forehead.

"You did good, baby. You're very bad ass. You haven't been an Einherja for long, and you have more kills than some veterans." He carried Serena to the car and buckled her into the front seat. She tried to raise her arms.

*Badass Barista wins again.*

Her head started spinning again, and her stomach felt woozy. "I don't feel so good. I really want to go back to the Sanctuary." She had a hard time trying not to mumble her words. Erik hopped into the car and sped down the street. "Erik? Are you listening to me?" Serena whispered. He slowed down the car and turned to look at her. "I really like you." Serena could have sworn she heard Erik say *I know.* She placed her head against the cool window. *That was too close.* The giant pine trees blurred together, and the bumpy ride lulled her to sleep.

Serena wasn't sure how long she was asleep for, but she knew exactly where she was. *I can smell his cinnamon soap.* Her raspy voice mumbled, "Your soap always makes you smell like cinnamon. It makes me want to eat oatmeal cookies. I just love cookies." She grinned, slowly opening her eyes. "It feels so good to be back here."

Erik sat on the edge of the bed, gently rubbing her leg. "Serena, you can't do that to me. You're going to get yourself killed. You need to be more careful."

She sluggishly sat up. "I know. I wanted to protect Aimee and try to save that girl. But I failed, and now someone else is dead." Serena's stomach twirled into a knot as her heart began to sink. The darkness began to creep through her body.

*If only I was faster…maybe if I'd seen them ten minutes sooner. Maybe she would still be alive…* Erik grabbed hold of her shoulders and gave her whole body a shake.

"Hey! I know that feeling—if only you were faster, or stronger, or you had more time. Listen—you did the best you could. Sometimes you can't save everyone. All right?"

Serena grabbed his hand and placed it above her heart. "I know. It just hurts, and I feel disappointed in myself. I don't want anyone to die, especially if we're meant to protect them."

He pulled Serena's hands off her chest and placed them on his knee, outlining her knuckles. "We can only try to do our best, and sometimes it doesn't work out. Aimee told me this wasn't your first time encountering these robed men. The night I came back to the Sanctuary, your neck was covered in fresh bruises. That was from fighting one of them, wasn't it?"

Serena slowly nodded as she fidgeted her fingers. "The night before you came back, I was attacked in my house. I killed one of the robed man in my bedroom. He said the Goddess would be pleased he'd found me. And then, last night, they told me the Goddess wouldn't care if they cut me up a bit." Erik's eyebrows creased and his lips tightened.

"I am not sure which goddess would want this. There are several they could sacrifice to."

Serena shrugged. "When I fell asleep after I killed that first man, I had this dream where he found me in Avonmore Park; he said a god's blood would spill. They mean to sacrifice someone with a god's blood. I don't know what this is going to accomplish. They're going to try to sacrifice me, especially now I've killed three of them."

She noticed Erik's skin was almost ghoulish, with dark circles surrounding his eyes. She wouldn't put it past him to stay awake all night watching her. He grabbed her wrists.

"This has to be the last time you leave without me until we figure out how to stop these attacks. Confronting you twice is no coincidence. They need the blood of a god; we all need to be more careful. Aidan and Gamble are in the library looking through the books to see if they can figure out what kind of demon these robed men are. Listen, you really need to rest to recover after that fight, and I have a meeting in my office. I mean it, Serena. Don't leave again."

She pulled his hand off, gently rubbing in between his knuckles. "You can stop worrying; I'm not going to let them kill me. Until this is over, I won't leave the Sanctuary without you again, I promise. But you need to relax and get some sleep. You look like death."

He bent down, giving her a quick peck on the cheek, and whispered in her ear. "I really like you, Serena Annar. Always and forever. I will sleep after I find some answers."

Serena slowly closed both eyes, letting out a soft moan. She whispered, "You're crazy; I love sleep." She could hear Erik laughing all the way out the door.

She slept for what seemed like hours. When she finally woke up, she stretched out both legs and slowly got out of bed, wondering where everybody was.

A pile of clothes was neatly folded next to the bed. Serena struggled to slip on a black sundress as her whole body screamed in pain. The cuts on her shoulder felt as if someone were poking them with a hot iron. She looked down at her shoulder, which was covered in a cream gauze stained with deep red around the edges. "I really need to be careful next time." As she walked through the door, her throbbing ankle gave away and she fell into the hallway. *Why am I getting out of bed again?*

Justice rushed down the hall and wrapped an arm around her shoulder, pulling her back up onto her feet.

"You should be resting. Why are you out of bed?" A *tsk* came from his mouth, and Serena let out a deep breath.

"You're the one to talk—you just woke up from being unconscious. I felt like I needed to get out of that room for a bit. I'm not sure it was the best idea, but I'm already out of bed."

His face relaxed as he snorted. "I understand how you feel. Aimee keeps trying to lock me in her room." Serena giggled. "I need to thank you for protecting her and our baby."

She nodded as Justice helped her down each step. "She's one of my only friends. I'll try to always protect them the best I can. Did you guys tell Erik?"

Justice shook his head. "Not yet, but we will soon. When the time is right."

Erik briskly walked to the duo, and wrapped his arm around Serena's other shoulder. He stared down at Justice. "Did you tell Erik what?"

Justice cleared his throat and announced, "Erik's girlfriend happens to be in the lead with Aimee for best girlfriend of the year!" The Einherja clapped and cheered from their various places at the library's tables. *Nice save, Justice.* Serena rolled her eyes. "You guys are ridiculous; any of you would have done the same thing." Erik helped Serena sit down next to Aimee, before heading around one of the bookshelves and pulling out a whiteboard.

Dawn pulled out a black dry erase marker out of his pocket, handing it to Erik. "All right, everyone—we need to pull our resources together and find out what we are dealing with." He uncapped the marker and began to write. "This is what we know so far. We have demonic robed men that turn into black puddles when they die. They are taking people and sacrificing them on top of pentagrams. They have mentioned a goddess."

Aidan stood up. "This is going to be difficult to narrow down. There are several hundreds of possibilities, from what Serena has said. They must believe that this goddess is not in Valhalla, but a living being."

Serena lifted her hand up. "I have a question. What is

Valhalla?" Everyone froze and stared at her. She opened her hands in front of her body "What? I'm still learning, remember?"

Aidan cleared his throat. "Valhalla is the hall of the fallen. All who uphold the law of Odin in life and death will be guided through the golden doors by Valkyries. Then, you will join your ancestors until the day you are reborn." Serena could feel the intensity of Erik's stare. He looked as though he was memorizing her face. She did a quick once over brush of her face. *No zit.* Erik beamed towards her. "Is there anything else we are missing?" After a few minutes he turned away, and Serena's shoulders relaxed.

As Serena tried to think of something that could help, she remembered the ground shaking violently. Serena muttered, "Of course, why didn't I think about it before? The earthquakes." Erik raised his eyebrow, running a hand over his stubbly chin.

Serena cleared her throat and spoke up. "The earthquakes; they are connected to this. Avonmore never has this many— especially so close to one another."

Erik nodded. "You're right, Serena. This is what we are going to do. Aidan and Gamble—continue looking through our books. Try to find something about these robed men, and make a list of some possible goddesses. Justice—take Aimee to Eldamar and see if her uncle can let you access the Alfheim archives. I will take Serena to Vanir and look through the elder's archives." Erik turned towards Dawn. "Dawn, you're in charge while I am gone. If anyone finds anything, come back to the Sanctuary and leave a note by the attic portal. I will check it regularly."

Aidan moved to the next table as Gamble grabbed a pile of books, throwing them down. As he began to flip through the pages of a dusty book, he looked up, turning towards everyone. "Good luck, guys."

Justice and Aimee said goodbye to everyone and headed

towards the mirror portal in the front entry. Erik sat down next to Serena. "Well, we can leave tomorrow morning, if your ankle feels better. Vanir is the capital city of Vanaheim. This is the realm where all the Elders live, and where the head institute of all the Sanctuary is. I have a couple of things I need to take care of before we go—will you be okay getting back upstairs?"

She nodded. "I'll be fine. I can always ask one of these guys for help if I need to." Before Erik left the library, he patted Aidan and Gamble on their backs.

"Hey, Aidan and Gamble, pass me a couple of books. I'll try to see if I can help."

Aidan gave Serena a toothy grin. "Thanks. There are a lot of boring books we have to go through. Gamble and I are always stuck on book duty."

"I know." Serena nodded. "But I think it is Erik's way of trying to protect both of you. He takes his fatherly role very seriously."

Gamble rolled his eyes. "We know. It just gets old after a while."

After a couple of hours of reading about demons with no leads, Gamble organized the books on top of the table while Aidan put some back in their rightful places. "Do you need help to go back to your room?"

Serena shook her head. "No; thanks anyway." *Time for the Scooby Gang to hit the books.*

He nodded as they both headed up the stairs. "Goodnight, Serena." She opened the next book and blew the dust off the pages. "Demonology throughout the ages. Sounds very interesting." Letting out loud sigh, she flipped through the pages. They were filled with black and white drawings of every sort of demon. Serena rubbed her eyes and yawned. She placed her head down on the thick, dusty book and fell asleep.

Serena floated up over the table. She looked down, and saw her body lying down on the book sleeping. "Wow. I feel so airy. What was that word again to describe this?" She snapped her fingers. "Oh yes. Astral projection."

Dawn hurried down the stairs while holding a piece of paper which was sealed by red wax. Serena swooshed closer to the boy, trying to get a better look at the red seal. "What are you doing, Dawn? What's up with that seal?" He walked up to Serena's sleeping body and poked her arm.

"Serena...are you awake?" Serena rolled her eyes. "Obviously not. There is drool steeping out of my mouth." He waited a couple of minutes, watching her, and finally walked out the door. Serena followed closely behind him. He stopped at the mirror in the front entry, whispered *"Vanir"*, and threw a piece of paper into the portal.

Serena jerked back up as Dawn entered the library. "Hey Dawn, what are you doing up so late?"

He looked around nervously and swallowed. "I couldn't fall asleep, so I went for a little walk. Goodnight, Serena. Have a good visit to Vanir."

She limped the whole way back to her bedroom. Pulling out her purple backpack from the closet, Serena grabbed some clothes and shoes. As she dug through the clothes, she found a cream tension wrap buried deep in the socks. She sat down on her bed and wrapped her ankle. *Why would Dawn lie to me?* Letting out a big yawn, she flung herself down on the bed and fell back to sleep.

After a couple hours' restless sleep, Serena got up and slipped on a long-sleeve green shirt and black yoga pants. Reaching underneath the bed, her hand moved all around the hardwood floor. "Where is it? I can't go to Vanir unarmed—especially since that is where Henrik lives." Serena bent down, peering underneath the bed. "Erik must have it."

As she slipped on her backpack, he strolled through the bedroom door. In his hand was her belt with the two daggers. "Don't worry—I wouldn't let you go unarmed." He lifted her shirt up and securely wrapped the belt around her waist, his cold hands brushing her stomach. Serena shivered as goose-bumps rose.

"Thank you, Mr. Baldr. You are looking very sharp and prepared." Erik's sword was securely strapped onto his back, along with a belt with a couple of daggers. He winked and gave her a sly smile.

"I want to be ready for anything. Let's go to Vanir. Ready?" Erik asked as they headed up to the attic. Serena nodded as they walked through into the swirling blue light. Quickly, she grabbed Erik's arm.

"I don't think I will ever get used to this suctioning feeling. I feel like I am going to be sucked up into a vortex and be stuck forever in the space-time continuum."

Erik's entire body began to shake, and he burst with uncontrollable laughter. "Serena, you are being so paranoid. I don't think that is a really thing. Or...maybe it is." Erik pulled Serena's hands off his arm and gave her a slight push. Serena's face dropped and she grabbed on to his arm again.

"That was not funny." She let out a nervous chuckle. Her nerves felt shaken to the core; what would happen if she was stuck in there forever? "Maybe it was a little funny. But I would not like to be trapped in here."

Erik pointed to the end of the blue light. "Well, you won't be stuck in here. There is the door to Vanir." He pulled open the dark grey stone door, and bowed his head down "After you, my paranoid lady."

Serena scurried through the portal. "Finally, out of that vortex trap."

Erik shook his head. "I have never heard anyone describe the portals as you do."

She grinned. "I am one of a kind."

# CHAPTER NINE

HAND IN HAND, THEY WALKED THROUGH THE DOOR, A WAVE OF warm air swirling around the duo. Unlike the humid warmth of Alfheim, Vanaheim felt like a desert. Serena froze in the middle of the street. "I didn't know what to expect. Vanir is incredible." She swung around, attempting to take in all the sights. The buildings were all closely packed together, each one made of brown stone with runes beautifully carved into them. Serena walked towards a large building, tracing the swirling symbols with a fingertip. "What are all these symbols?"

Erik followed her hand with his. "They are runes—very scared to the descendants. The tree of life, Yggdrasil, was located in Asgard. To obtain its knowledge, Odin hung and speared himself against a branch. He hung on that tree for nine days, forbidding any god to help him. On the tenth day, the tree revived Odin and presented him with these runes for his suffering, filled with the secrets of the universe."

Serena continued to shadow the runes. "He sounds like a very brave and powerful god, sacrificing himself for the greater good."

"That he is. He is the King of the Aesir gods, of war and death. The one-eyed raven-god."

Serena didn't recognize the beautiful dark green trees grew along the streets. She assumed they were a species only found in this realm. Vines whipped from their trunks, climbing up some of the building sides. The last of the bridges connecting the buildings was completely overgrown with moss. Serena ran her hand against its softness. "It's as if someone painted all this moss everywhere."

Erik glanced around. "I am not sure how long it's been like this. I haven't it seen it any other way." Continuing down the street, wild flowers began taking over, even growing out of each and every crack along the way. Pale yellow finches darted through the skies, chirping merrily to one another. If Serena could describe this place, she would call it paradise.

On a side street, hundreds of people gathered in a market crowded with wooden stalls. Serena saw elves of every color you could imagine—and even a few she didn't know. Children ran up and down the streets, screaming merrily, kicking a leather-bound ball. Three hefty bearded men sat on wooden boxes, strumming on their guitars, filling the air with soothing music.

An elderly woman came towards Serena and handed her a sticky roll, closing her fingers around it. "Make sure someone doesn't steal it." Serena raised her eyebrow and slightly nodded.

Taking a big bite, she grinned towards the lady. "Thank you!"

Erik reached into his pocket and handed the woman some change. She waved goodbye as she swung her wooden basket full of treats.

"There are a lot of sights to take in. I just can't get over it."

Erik looked around. "Vanir is a very alive city. There are always markets or festivals. In a couple of months, I will bring you back for the celebration of the Summer Solstice.

There will be a huge festival just outside the city. It is one of few times of the year the Elven council and Elders come together. Alfheim and Vanaheim do most of their trade that day."

They continued walking up the street, finally reaching a large, stone bridge. On each side stood two huge stone statues. Erik pointed to the one on the left. "That is Odin." Odin wore armour painted in gold and in his right hand he held a spear. He had a long beard and was missing one eye. On the top of his head was a helmet with two long horns sticking out. Serena stared up at the massive statue. "Why does he only have one eye?"

"There once was a well of wisdom, Mirmir, located in the realm of Jotunheim. Odin sacrificed his eye to gain the knowledge of the past, present and future."

Serena pressed her lips together. "Can I ask you something you might find offensive?"

Erik leaned towards her "Of course. I don't mind answering any of your questions."

Serena gave him a half-smile. "If Odin knew all the secrets of the universe and had gained the knowledge of the past, present and future, why did he let himself get swallowed up by Fenrir?"

Erik parted his lips slightly. "That is not an offensive question; it's actually quiet brilliant. Odin, with his knowledge of the future, knew the outcome of the Ragnarok War. He knew many would die, but they would kill a lot of the forces of evil, saving humanity in the process. His consolation was foreknowledge that a new era of peace between the descendants of the Aesir gods and elves would come out of the war—a new, powerful alliance rising out of the sea."

Erik pointed to the two ravens sitting on top of Odin's shoulders. "Those two ravens are believed to be Huginn and Muninn. They would travel across the realms and bring information back to him. They have been perched on top of Odin's statue ever since it has been built. If someone tries to take them off or disrupts Odin, they will attack. Over the years, a couple of schoolboys have lost an eye or two."

He pulled out a bag of sunflower seeds out of his pocket, offering it towards Serena. "Every year for the Yule celebrations, the two ravens disappear. The legend is that they fly to Valhalla to visit Odin and bring him the news from that year."

Serena grabbed a handful of the seeds and threw them up into the air. The two ravens squawked loudly as they caught the seeds with their piercing black beaks. "What is the Yule?" Erik grabbed a handful of seeds and threw it up towards the birds. "The Yule is a twelve-day celebration beginning on the Winter solstice. Like twelve days of straight Christmas."

*What?*

Her inner child screamed and cheered. Christmas always was her favorite holiday. "Yule sounds amazing!"

Erik let out a deep chuckle. "Yes, it is a lot of fun. I am excited to have someone to celebrate everything with." Serena's cheeks flushed as she lightly pushed Erik.

*What a sap!*

As though he could read her mind, Erik grabbed Serena by the waist twirled her around. She threw her head back laughing. He lowered her until her feet touched the ground. Serena looked around to see if anyone was watching them. A couple of women were across the road, kneeling and praying to the next statue. They were giggling as they watched the couple. As her cheeks continued to flush, Serena tried to hide her face behind both hands.

Erik ran a hand through his wispy black hair. "Well, better stop embarrassing ourselves in front of the gods—but I am sure they enjoy the entertainment."

Serena let out an exasperated sigh. "I'm sure they're just loving this."

Walking across the road, he pointed to the statue on the right. "Now, that is Odin's beautiful wife, Frigg, goddess of love and marriage." She wore a golden dress that wrapped around the bottom of the bridge, going all the way down to the water. Her curly hair followed the dress, and in her hands, she held a giant sword. She was breathtaking.

The giggling women continued to kneel at the bottom of Frigg and laid beautiful flowers down on her feet. The closer Serena walked towards the statue, she could hear what the women were saying. "Frigg, bless our home with laughter, love and song. Keep our family strong." Serena picked up a couple of blue flowers near the bridge and kneeled in front of Frigg. She gently placed the flowers on top of the stone feet. A warm breeze wrapped around her, like a blanket on a cool day. A sweet voice whispered through the wind. *Daughter of Nótt.* The two women stopped praying and stared at Serena. No one said a word.

Serena shuffled back to Erik. *Both of those women heard that voice...I am not crazy!*

Erik entwined his fingers with hers as they made their way across the stone bridge. Serena ran to the edge, peering down at the clearest green water. She couldn't believe her eyes and shook her head. "I don't understand how everything here could be so beautiful and magical. I wouldn't think a place like this could ever exist." Erik smiled with sadness in his eyes. "Even though we came here in not the best circumstances, I am happy I got to bring you to Vanaheim. I forgot how beautiful Vanir is. Seeing your face, taking in all the sights, makes me forget about all the ugly memories."

She squeezed his hand. "Well, we can try to make happy memories here. I'm sure your mother would want that."

His eyes were glued to the water, watching the waves crash together. "I know you are right. She wouldn't want me to dwell on the past." They watched the water together for a few moments in silence, enjoying the rippling dark shadow looming over the water.

The skyline was blocked by a large hill covered in stone

buildings and houses. At the top was an extravagant dark stone castle. It had many tall towers, with dark blue domes and windows made of deep red stained glass. She imagined Dracula would have lived in a castle similar to this one. Even though Vanir was colorful and beautiful, there was something off about the castle—like it hid many secrets.

"That is where the Elders live, and where the Guardians train. Deep underneath the castle is the Fengsel, where the Elders keep the most dangerous criminals, guarded by their vicious lap dogs, the Berserkers." Serena shivered shifting uncomfortably. It must be horrible to be trapped underneath that hill, stuck in the dark will all those spiders and creepy bugs. *Ick!* "The Elders shove as many prisoners as they can in there. Most people who end up there die and are forgotten, or the Berserkers torture them until they beg to be killed."

Serena frowned. "Doesn't anyone care about the people in there? How do you know they actually deserve to be locked up?" Erik shook his head. "No one cares. The Elders have been running Vanaheim like this for centuries. The people don't want to know what happens in there, so they don't ask any questions. If one of their loved ones gets arrested, they just push it out of their minds." That statement did not sit well with Serena. What about justice and fair trials?

"From what I've seen of your father, it seems like the Elders are corrupt and vicious. How can people live like this? I bet many of those prisoners don't deserve that kind of treatment."

Erik continued to stare at the hill. "You are right. But people are afraid of the Elders. No one will rise against them."

The couple continued up the steep hill until they reached a grand door made of dark mahogany wood with golden swirls. A male dark elf rushed through the door. Avoiding any eye contact, he quickly looked down at floor. "M...M...

Master Baldr, I wasn't aware you were planning a visit." Erik placed his hand on the dark elf's shoulder. He winced a bit.

"Haewon, it's fine. It was a spur of the moment visit. And I have told you plenty of times—just call me Erik. Serena, this is Nathaniel and Milia's oldest son, Haewon." Haewon bowed his head even lower.

"Nice to meet you, Haewon. You have wonderful parents —they're quite the cooks!"

As he looked up at Serena's face, his dark grey eyes twinkled. "It is nice to meet you as well, Miss Serena. My parents have spoken very highly of you. Will Miss Serena require a room?"

Erik shook his head. "No thank you, Haewon. She will be staying in my room. That is all." Haewon nodded and scurried off, disappearing down into the hallway.

The front entrance was surrounded by paintings of Odin and Frigg. Lit candles hung off the walls, and an enormous chandelier with hundreds of lights and crystals dangled off the ceiling. A giant staircase with a swirled gold railing stood in the middle of the room. Many people shuffled in and out of the castle; for a moment, Erik and Serena watched the commotion. The couple began to trek up the winding staircase. Two girls were descending, whispering. As soon as they saw them, both stopped talking and stared at Erik. The girl closest to Serena had long blonde hair and a face that looked like she'd sucked on a lemon. She purposefully slammed her shoulder into Serena's side. The second girl had a black pixie haircut and a chubby waistline; she covered her mouth and snickered.

Serena held in her tongue, even though it was hard. She knew the slam was intentional. The girl turned around, glaring at Serena. For just a moment, her blue eyes flashed deep blood red.

"You don't deserve to be here, half-breed."

Serena's blood began to boil as she clenched her fist. That

was it; she couldn't hold her mouth any longer. "How can you say that? You don't even know who I am." The girl smirked as her pointy nose crinkled up. "Oh, I know exactly who you are, Daughter of Nótt. I have heard plenty about you from Elder Henrik."

Erik tried to pull her back, but Serena wouldn't have it. "Because he is *such* a reputable source." Serena gave the girl a thumbs-up. "Good job! Way to hang out with the cream of the crop." *Who was this girl?* The chubby girl crossed her arms, narrowing both eyes her body leaned forward and for a moment Serena thought she was going to pounce.

"Come on Nina, let's not waste any more time on her. We have much better things to do with our time."

Serena nodded. "I agree, Nina. You should leave."

But before she turned to follow her friend down the stairs. "Your time is almost up, half-breed."

As the girls reached the bottom, they laughed obnoxiously loudly. Serena was flabbergasted. "What?"

"I wouldn't worry about her." Erik shrugged. "My father was trying to arrange a marriage between Justice and Nina. She is a bit socially inept." Serena stared down the stairs and watched the two girls disappear into the hallway.

"I've never seen red eyes like hers before."

Erik looked confused. His mouth opened as if to say something but nothing came out.

The couple reached the third floor, and walked to the end of the hallway through a dark wooden door. "Welcome to my second home."

A humongous bed was pushed against the wall, covered in fur blankets. A painting of his mother hung above his bed, and a bronze bath was in the corner of the room, covered in gold swirls. Serena's eyes went big as her mouth dropped. "Geez, I'm glad I sold my house before you could see it. It's a mud hut compared to your one room."

Erik sat down at his desk, which overlooked the window.

He had stacks of papers and books scattered on the desk top. "My family has always had beautiful things. Baldr was the shinning god—the god of beauty and light. It's my family's obsession."

Serena rolled her eyes and Erik cleared his throat. "I am sure I would have loved your house. This room was a parting gift from my mother. She had it decorated."

Serena gave him a half-smile. "I guess I can't seem to say this enough, but your mother seemed to love you and Justice so much."

Erik pushed aside the mountain of papers. "She did. I just wished she could have met you."

"I wish I could have as well." *Even though technically, I have met her. But that is a whole other conversation for another time.*

Serena placed the backpack on the hardwood floor and went towards the desk. Seeing a frame sticking out of the papers, she pulled it out. It was a picture of Erik holding Justice when he was a newborn, with the sweetest smile on his face. She took it away from the desk and put it on top of his nightstand. "That's a much better place for this picture instead of being buried underneath all your papers."

Erik stood up and rubbed her shoulders "How are you feeling?"

Serena kept her eyes on the picture. "I'm fine. Still a little sore, but it's nothing to worry about." He massaged her shoulders, then walked towards the bathtub. He turned on the taps.

"Well, I have a couple of things I need to do, so just have a nice hot bath and relax. I should be back in an hour or so."

Serena strolled towards the bath, dipping her hand down into the warm water. "I guess you're right. I should try to relax." She slowly started to undress, and folded her clothes into a pile. She grabbed a white robe from Erik's chair and quickly wrapped her body in its soft material. Erik looked as though he had seen an angel. *Awestruck* was how Serena would describe it. Erik took a deep breath.

"You are making it hard to leave. I will be back soon." He kissed her on the cheek as she exaggerated her eye roll.

"Get out of here. Stop gawking and let me have my bath." Erik blew a kiss before he left the room.

After hanging the robe up, Serena eased herself down into the bath. She scrubbed her hair and body with the lavender soap which sat on the side of the tub, before laying her head down on the white bath pillow and enjoying the feel of the warm water surrounding her body. She closed her eyes for only what seemed to be a minute, and gentle knock came from the door. "Really? Of course, right when I become so comfortable." Serena got out of the bath, wrapping herself in a soft purple towel.

Opening the door a crack, a beautiful dark elf with long teal hair stood patiently outside, and in her hand was a black garment bag. "Hello Miss Serena. Master Baldr has sent me to bring you this dress."

Serena opened the door wide. "Please come in. Sorry for only being wrapped in a towel."

"It's no trouble at all, miss. I am Elva, I am one of the chamber maids for the Baldr family. I also work as a seamstress. Master Erik has asked me to bring this dress to you and take you to meet him for supper." *What? Doesn't he know I brought clothes with me?*

Elva unzipped the black bag and pulled out a long, silky gown, dark forest green, with a silt on the side. "It's perfect for you, miss. The green will make your beautiful eyes glow." She wasn't wrong about the dress, but Serena really didn't want to wear it. Instead, she grabbed the bag and placed it down on top of the bed. Pulling out her back pack, she hurled the clothes out until she found a navy polka dot dress.

She slipped on the dress, and took a once over look in the

mirror. Her hair began its wild ways, it frizzed and curled at the end. "Look at this jungle!"

The elf cleared her throat. "Would you like me to help with your hair?" Serena nodded; she never really was good at making her hair cooperate. But Elva had no problem as she twisted the brown curls and pinned them into a voluminous updo.

Elva smiled looking at her work. "You look beautiful, Miss Serena." Before the duo left the room, Serena slipped on her favorite pair of red flats. "Master Erik is awaiting you." The elf took Serena up another flight of stairs, proceeding through the long hallway. The walls were filled with long candle torches. Reaching the end of the hall, Elva opened the door for Serena. "Just through this door, Miss Serena. Have a lovely evening." Serena quickly hugged the elf. "Thank you, Elva. I hope to see you again." Elva smiled and went back down the hall.

Serena walked onto a stone balcony. Purple rose petals were sprinkled all over the floor. She followed the rose petals until she reached Erik, standing in front of a wooden table covered in long candlesticks. He wore a deep forest green button down shirt and black dress pants. *Oh God, he is matching the dress.* In his hands, Erik held a bouquet of deep red roses. He handed it to Serena and gave her a kiss on the cheek. "You are not wearing the dress."

"Nope. I like this dress; it's comfortable." She twirled around. "And it looks amazing with my red shoes."

He simply agreed. "You do look beautiful."

He pulled out her chair and she sat down. "This is very romantic."

Erik sat down across the table. He reached out past the candles and held her hand. "This was my mother's favorite part of the castle. She would always bring Justice and I up here when we were younger. During the day, we have the perfect view of the busy little town and the green river." Two dark elves came onto the balcony, carrying a ham and pineapple pizza with hot peppers. Serena laughed.

"How did you know that is my favorite pizza?"

Erik smiled. "Aimee told me."

The couple ate in silence until the entire pizza was consumed. "Those dark elves definitely know how to make a good pizza."

Erik agreed. "I have something to say to you, and I don't want you to panic." Serena straightened up and her eyes grew big. "Okay..." *What could be so important?*

"I think I love you and I would like you to protect my mother's ring." His voice became shaky; Serena would have sworn she saw a single drop of sweat roll down his face. "Uhh...I'm not asking you to marry me. Don't freak out." Erik's voice went quiet, she barely heard what he was saying.

She couldn't help but chuckle. "I think I love you as well."

Erik held his breath and nodded.

Serena had seen the girls at her high school get such rings from boys but Serena had never been so lucky.

His shoulders relaxed and took a deep breath in. His hand rummaged through his pocket and Erik pulled out a white gold ring with a lavender diamond onto her finger. "I didn't want to scare you away."

"You haven't." She jumped off the seat and hugged Erik. "This ring is so beautiful."

"I don't think anyone else deserves it as much as you do."

Serena rolled her eyes. She had never met anyone so cheesy but romantic. It was like one of those old romantic movies she would watch late at night with her mom.

"You are a cheesy man but I happen to love it. Cheese is great!"

The couple walked hand in hand back towards the room. "Is there any food you don't like?"

That was a difficult question. Serena had to think about it for a moment. "Hmmm. Asparagus and liquorice." He stopped in the middle of the hallway, causing Serena to be pulled back. "I don't believe you. You are the only person I know who is obsessed with food and coffee." She wasn't sure how to take that comment.

Serena pinched the side of his waist, trying to grasp whatever extra fat he had. "Hey! There is nothing wrong with loving food or coffee." She ran both hands down the side of her body. "I just need a lot of food to upkeep my womanly figure, thank you very much."

Erik roared with laughter as he scooped up Serena and twirled her around. "And what a nice soft figure you have indeed."

"I'm not going to lie—that sounded a bit creepy. You're lucky I like you."

Erik stuck his tongue out at her. "I am a very lucky man." Without any effort, Erik threw Serena over his shoulder and carried her the whole way back to the room. He flopped her down on the bed and lay down next to her.

"How's your shoulder?" Serena laughed. "I bet it feels a bit numb."

Erik puffed out his chest and flexed his arm. "Not after carrying a dainty little woman like you." Serena scoffed as if she were insulted. "In no reality or realm am I dainty. I'm hardy, like an ox."

Erik tilted his head towards Serena, and raised his eyebrows. "Did you just compare yourself to an ox?"

Serena sat up and beamed. "I sure did. Those animals are bad ass power machines, pulling charts and wagons."

Erik patted her shoulder. "You are pretty bad ass."

Serena nodded. "I'm glad we agree."

# CHAPTER TEN

THE SMELL OF FRESHLY BREWED COFFEE JOLTED SERENA UP.
"Dreams really do come true—freshly brewed coffee and a
handsome man serving me. I could get used to this." Erik
poured a cup of coffee and handed her a giant fluffy blue-
berry muffin.

"That's right," Erik laughed. "I am a genie and I grant
coffee wishes." The smooth caramel smell wrapped around
her like a warm blanket on a cool day. The nutty aroma
tickled her nose.

"Let's go to the archives today to see if we can find
anything—or maybe the scholars will know something."

Serena nodded and finished her muffin. She took off her
dress and gently placed it next to the purple backpack. "I
forgot to say thank you for the beautiful dress, but I like
buying my own clothes, so you don't have to do it." She
slipped on a t-shirt and her favorite pair of black legging
capris.

"Okay." His voice stammered. The silence was thick,
Serena avoided his glances and thought maybe she'd made a
mistake about bringing up the dress.

Erik broke the silence. "I often get custom costumes made

for the Summer Solstice festival. There is always a contest for the best costume. We have long-time rivalry with the London Sanctuary."

The thought of Erik in an assortment of animal costumes ran through her head. "Cool! Everyone deserves a little break from that responsibility of protecting the whole planet." Serena clicked her heels together after slipping on the worn red flats.

"I agree. When we all have time off, we go a bit crazy and let loose. One year, we dressed up as the London Sanctuary. Funny thing is, they had the same idea and dressed up as us. That was the only year in the whole history of the costume contest that two groups tied."

They went up the giant staircase until they reached the seventh floor. The couple walked into the musty room; each way Serena looked had never-ending shelves filled with books. Scurrying all around the room, moving books back and forth, were stumpy men with beards of every colour, and matching robes.

"Erik, are these scholars dwarves?"

He nodded. "Yes—the dwarves are mainly scholars or blacksmiths."

Serena watched a dwarf climb up a metal rolling ladder as another pushed him into another aisle. *I would have too much fun.* She began to laugh but was almost instantly hushed by an unknown source.

An older dwarf with a scraggly white beard that reached his stomach, and arms filled with books, motioned for Erik to follow. He placed the pile on top of a metal round table. "Hello, Master Erik, I am scholar Mordus. I have procured some books that I think would be helpful."

They sat down and the dwarf opened a dusty black book. Serena ran her finger across one of the inscriptions. "This is the *Bok av døde*, a very powerful grimoire filled with black spells, demons and gods. I had to petition the Elders to unseal one of our vaults of forbidden books. Your father put up quite a fight for you not to be able to view it." Erik's eye flinched.

"This book must be the one. If not, I don't know where else to look."

The dwarf agreed. "We have Hekate, the goddess of necromancy, ghosts and sorcery. It has been many years since a cult has worshipped her; her cult was not known for sacrificing humans. They would occasionally sacrifice dogs at a crossroad. Were the humans found at a crossroad?" Serena shook her head. "No crossroads in Avonmore. The town is basically one large circle." Mordus ran his hand through his white beard.

He continued to flip through the pages, stopping at a picture of a giant blue woman with four arms and long, black, wavy hair. She had a long tongue sticking out of her mouth and an extra eye on her forehead. In each hand, she held a different type of weapon. "This is the demon goddess Kali. She is the goddess of death. The cult mainly sacrificed people by strangulation or by drowning them."

Erik sighed "No drownings or strangulation were involved in these sacrifices. This seems a bit hopeless."

As the hours passed, the list of potential goddesses grew smaller. The dwarf took a deep breath, and his eyes drooped down in disappointment. "I am sorry, Master Erik; I was sure we could have narrowed down the list."

Mordus took the books that rested in the pile and began to put them back into the shelves. Serena continued to flip through the grimoire. *Please, Nótt, help me find the answer.* The pages began to blur together, until one swiped the tip of her finger. "Ouch!" She stuck her finger in her mouth to get rid of the blood. "That was very convenient; could have saved a couple hours!" *Well duh, Captain Obvious!*

Erik turned towards Serena. "What are you talking about?" She let out a nervous giggle. "It's nothing."

The drop of blood absorbed into the page, spreading

across one word: Hel. *The ruler of the underworld.* There was no picture—just a description. Serena cleared her throat and began to read. "Hel, the daughter of Loki. Punished as a child for Loki's trickery, she was sentenced to rule the underworld for all eternity. Odin suppressed her powers, and she was forbidden to enter any other realm."

As Serena closed her eyes, she had a flashback of the woman filling her mouth with maggots.

Serena placed a hand against her cheek. "I think I've found our answer." She tapped the page. "Erik, it's Hel."

Erik's eyes flickered down the page, stopping at the description. "How can you be so sure?"

"I can't explain it. I just have a feeling it's her."

"You might be right." Erik scrunched up his face and was silent for a moment. "Why would they sacrifice someone to Hel? What do they get out of this? But more importantly, what would Hel get out of this? I believe the scholars have a theory about her—they think her powers lie in the under-world. If she managed to come up to Earth, I don't know if her powers would work here. Odin did cast her out." His fingers tapped against the wooden table.

She shook her head. "In my dream, her powers seemed to work just fine. Hel will be coming to Earth—and soon." She shuddered at the thought of Hel's rotting arms and maggots. "We need to go back to the Sanctuary and tell the others what we found."

"Master Baldr, please wait a moment." A female dwarf with short red hair below her ears came running through the archives. She huffed while wiping a droplet of sweat off her shiny forehead. She bowed her head down towards the couple. "I am glad I finally caught up with you, Master Baldr. I am Viola, apprentice scholar. I have found a possible connec-tion with the dead ravens and the earthquakes. Please follow me."

They followed the young dwarf deeper into the archives.

In the small dark corner, she pointed to a wooden table with books scattered all around. "Please take a seat." She pulled out a worn book hidden underneath the biggest pile. "Are you aware of what happened after your ancestor, the Shining God, was killed?"

Erik had a puzzled look on his face. "Only parts. Frigg and Odin were overwhelmed with grief. The world wept after the death of Baldr."

Viola tapped on the books dusty golden cover. "Yes, of course the world suffered. But do you know what happened after that?" Erik shook his head. "I have found this book, *The Death of Baldr*. The Elders and scholars have buried it deep within the archives. After weeks of looking, I came across it and hid from the others." Viola flipped through the pages, stopping in the middle of the book. "It says Odin was distraught after the death of his favorite son. He ripped a hole through Midgard's core, trying to reach Muspelheim. When this happened, the balance of Midgard shifted, causing mass deaths of wildlife and plants. In the history of men, never has there been as many recorded earthquakes as there were in the 8th century. It was a time of great change across the world. But this is where it stops because someone ripped out the rest of the pages."

Erik twisted his mouth. "Of course they did. It seems the same thing is happening now in Avonmore."

Viola closed the book. "I have a theory, Master Erik. I believe Avonmore is in the middle of that very spot Odin ripped a hole through. It would explain why the veil has always been weak." Serena snapped her fingers. Viola flinched at the loud sound.

"Viola, you are a genius. Except, I think that this time someone is trying to break *out* of Muspelheim."

Viola frowned and a shiver passed her body. "Now that is a scary thought. I don't even want to imagine what kind of horrors are trying to escape." Viola handed the book to Erik, but he pushed it back. "Thank you, Viola. Could you keep this a secret and hide the book from the other scholars? I am afraid if I bring this back to the Sanctuary, my father might find out."

She took the book, hiding it underneath her white robe. "I will. There is a reason someone ripped out the pages, and I intend to find out who did."

He shook the dwarf's hand. "You did a great job. Please keep me informed if you find anything else." Viola bowed her head down, rushing out of the archives.

Erik offered his hand to Serena, and she entwined her fingers with his. "I bet I know exactly who took the pages."

He nodded as they walked through the archives. "Henrik. For some reason, he is trying to hide what happened with Odin and Baldr. In those pages must be the answer to why Hel is doing this. This is proof; it has to be her."

Just as the couple walked through the heavy metal doors, Henrik came rushing down the stairs. Erik pushed Serena back into the wall, trying to go unnoticed by his father. "Let's follow him to see where he is going." Erik whispered. They followed him out of the castle and continued down the hill. Every so often, Henrik turned around to see if anyone was following him. Luckily, each time Erik and Serena had a chance to hide around the side of a house or building. He turned into a dark alley and waited for a couple of minutes. A man hidden by a black robe appeared.

The alley filled with an unfortunately familiar putrid smell. Serena curled her lip up. *I have smelled enough rotting flesh to last a lifetime.* Turning to look at Erik, she mouthed, *What the hell?* Erik motioned Serena to follow him. They walked around the building, crouching against the wall, watching Henrik and the robed man. As they finished their conversation, Henrik left the alley. The robed man walked in the direction of the couple. Serena pulled out her daggers. The moment he stepped out of the alley, Erik lunged and slammed the man's head into the stone sidewalk. "*Åpne Veien.*" The blue swirling archway portal appeared, and he began to drag the unconscious man through. "Hurry, Serena —before he wakes up." She bolted through the portal and into the attic.

Serena ran down into the library. "Hello? Where is everyone?" Aidan and Gamble popped their heads out from behind their books. "Hurry! We captured one of the robed men—go to the attic and help Erik." She continued into the training room, grabbing a handful of thick ropes from a drawer. Running back, the three boys dragged the man down the stairs. Aidan grunted. "He doesn't look very heavy, but he really is."

Serena looped the thick rope around the man's wrists. "I know—I helped carry him through the portal. Someone is slacking on his Pilates."

Erik shook his head. "And you call *me* cheesy. You are the master of cheese, Serena Annar. You really don't have a filter."

Serena puffed her chest out. "Nope, sorry, I wasn't born with one those." Laughing to herself, she tightened the rope around the man's ankles. Aidan and Gamble stared at her. "What?" She shrugged. "Better to be safe, in case he wakes up." They continued to drag him into the dining room and down to the basement, where they shoved him into an empty cell, shackling him up on the wall.

Aidan slammed and locked the metal door. "Wow, this makes our job a lot easier. When he wakes up, we can start to interrogate him. Great job."

Serena stared into the cell. "I wouldn't say your job was easier; just less dusty."

Gamble laughed. "You always have something to say, don't you?" Serena began to open her mouth but Gamble raised his hand. "I know—I am sure you have a witty comeback."

Aidan smiled brightly. "Well, we were getting sick of being stuck on book duty."

Erik patted Aidan and Gamble on the shoulder. "Good job, boys. Go have a nice break. Thank you for all your hard work. I know it sucks, looking through all of those stuffy books." The boys disappeared out of the basement, running up the stairs.

"I'm going to beat you at *Call of Duty*, Aidan."

Aidan yelled back "Oh, please, in your dreams, Gamble."

Serena followed Erik out the basement. "Sometimes, I forget they're both just fifteen-year-old boys. There are times they act a lot older."

Erik nodded. "I hope this blows over soon. I don't like exposing them to much violence. I would like them to enjoy the teenage years and have the childhood I never had."

Serena shut the basement door behind her. Erik waved his hand in the air. "*Låse.*"

Serena flopped her body down onto a wooden chair as Erik came out of the kitchen holding two cups of tea and oatmeal cookies. She grabbed one cup and kissed him on the cheek. "Thank you. I needed this. And I really need to learn some basic spells."

Erik sat down, sipping his tea. "That is true. Once everything settles down and we aren't in major research mode, Aimee and Gamble will begin magic lessons for you."

Serena blew the steam out of her cup and hesitantly took a sip. Her face cringed. *Way too hot to drink right now.* "Erik, how did you know to follow your father?"

"Ever since my mother passed away, I have been investigating Henrik. I have always had this feeling that there was something more to him, something he has been hiding from the Elders. I think my mother found out and he killed her. I have been trying to gather evidence against him to bring to the Elders. The past year, he has been having secret meetings with these robed men. I haven't been able to gather much evidence through the meetings, just some words here and there—mainly about the goddess and preparing the sacrifices."

Serena thought about it for a while "How would he benefit from these fanatics? This doesn't make sense."

Erik shrugged. "I am not sure, but we will try to get some answers from that creature in the cell. I will send a message to Elva to send our belongings back to the Sanctuary. I will see you in the morning; I need to get some work done. Goodnight."

He kissed her forehead and went into his room. "Goodnight, Erik."

The next morning, while everyone was eating a bacon and egg breakfast, Justice and Aimee returned to the sanctuary. Serena gasped as they walked through the door into the dining room. "Whoa, Aimee, look at you. You are absolutely glowing. That dress is heavenly." Aimee wore a long white dress and beautiful purple flower crown. Justice wore a matching tunic and tan canvas pants. He had flowers dangling from his neck.

"Everyone, we would like your attention please. Aimee and I got married last night in Alfheim, and we are having a baby." Everyone stopped eating and cheered.

Erik lunged off the chair and hugged his brother tightly. "Wow…Uncle Erik. It has a nice ring to it." He cleared his throat and yelled towards Aimee's stomach. "Hear that, little buddy? Your uncle Erik is going to teach you all about swords and crossbows."

Serena laughed and gave his shoulder a gentle squeeze. "I think it's too early for the baby to hear you."

Aimee laughed. "This will be his first niece or nephew. He's allowed to be excited." Justice came up behind Aimee, wrapping his arms around her stomach. "First baby, but definitely not the last." He snuggled his face deep into Aimee's neck.

"Let's survive the first and *maybe* we will have another."

Justice shook his head. "Come on! I need more people to play basketball with."

Aimee rolled her eyes. "Hah. In your dreams, Mr. Baldr."

Serena cleared her throat. "Let's have a party! I think cocktails and, of course, mocktails for the expecting and underage are in order." Everyone agreed.

She pulled Aimee into the corner. "Well, let's see the ring." Aimee lifted her hand up and green runes were spiraling around her finger. "These are runes that connect Justice and me. They say *Evig Melethril*. It means *forever love* in Elvish."

Serena poked the runes. "Wow, that is really cool. What about the…?"

Aimee put her hands on top of her stomach. "What about the baby? It isn't like getting a human tattoo. It's just a bit of magic, that's all." Aimee wrapped her hands around Serena's. "I know we haven't known each other for very long, but I would like you to be the godmother."

Serena's face lit up; she couldn't think of anything else that would make her happier. "Of course."

"Would you like to hear about the ceremony?"

Serena eagerly nodded. "Yes. Spill!" Aimee rubbed her hands together. "Luckily, my uncle is the High Councillor, or I would have never been able to throw such a last-minute wedding together. We were married just outside of Eldamar, underneath a giant waterfall. I had a giant white lily bouquet. It was very simple—just how we wanted it. My uncle did our marriage blessings and finished with our rune spells."

Serena smiled "That sounds lovely."

Aimee nodded her head. "My uncle surprised us with this giant feast; it seemed like almost all of Eldamar was invited. We danced all night and Justice drank many glasses of wine with all the Elves. I am completely exhausted. I better go visit everyone else before we can crash."

"Sorry for hogging you. Go mingle. You make a beautiful bride."

Serena walked back to Erik. He smiled and kissed her on the forehead. "We really needed all this good news. What a morale booster."

As everyone surrounded Aimee and Justice, Serena saw Dawn sneak out of the dining room form the corner of her eye. She gently slipped away from Erik and followed him. Dawn crouched down, frantically writing on a page. He folded it and used the same wax seal as before. As Dawn stood up, Serena walked out from behind the corner. "Who are you sending that letter to?"

He sneered at her. "It's none of your business."

She lunged towards him, and he stepped to the side. Serena stumbled to the ground. "You forgot who trained you; I know all your tricks."

She quickly recovered, pulling out her dagger which lit the room with a bright white light. "Well now, that's something new. Henrik didn't tell me you had a relic. I recognize that dagger. It's Natt, isn't it?" He began circling around her and every so often lunging at the dagger. Each time, Serena managed to dodge, and she charged at Dawn, grazing his arm.

"It is Natt. Nótt blessed me with it. It could have been you who received it, but I guess you're so much like your descendant, Dellinger—betraying the ones you supposedly love. Funny how history repeats itself."

Dawn's blue eyes flared as he jumped towards her. "What do you know about love, Serena? You fall in love with the first man who pays any attention to you. You are like a sad little puppy without him. That is not love—it's just pathetic."

Serena laughed while dodging his attack. "You know, it doesn't have to be like this, Dawn. All those people in there love you. You've been Justice's best friend since you were ten. There's still time to turn this around."

Zig zagging towards Serena, he grabbed her arm and flipped her over onto the ground. "This is why I am doing this: to protect him from his destiny. If he cooperates, Henrik will let him live." He kicked her in the chest. A sickening crunch followed. She tried to take a deep breath, but felt as if her bones would crumble at any minute.

"You don't get it, do you? Justice and Erik are destined for greatness. It is in their blood. Blessed by Odin, as they say. Powerful people want what they have and will stop at nothing. You stupid self-centered girl, thinking this is all about you. You are just going to get in the way. One of them will die, saving their precious *daughter of the night.*" As Serena pulled up on her knees, he kicked her back down again. She lifted Natt, trying to stab as hard as she could into his calf. Dawn screamed as blood ran down his leg.

He pulled out the dagger and threw it against the wall, before dragging his bleeding leg towards the portal. Dawn waved his hand in front of the portal. "*Vanir.*" Serena slowly got back up, her ribs throbbing in her chest. As she tried to breathe in, the pain pushed her back down.

"Please, Dawn, don't do this. You'll get us all killed. Henrik is a liar, and he will kill Justice. He will kill all your friends."

He shook his head. "No. Henrik promised me he wouldn't hurt Justice again."

Justice and Erik walked into the front entry. Dawn looked at Justice. "Sorry, brother." Without another word, he jumped into the portal. "No, Dawn. Don't do it!" Serena bellowed after him.

The brothers rushed to her side while Erik kneeled in front of Serena. "What is going on? Why did Dawn attack you?"

Serena tried to sit up which made her wince as her ribs continued to throb. "He's working for Henrik. I followed him here; I tried to stop him sending your father a note. Henrik will know about the baby, the wedding...He will know every-thing. He will definitely try to kill Aimee."

"NO!" Justice violently shook his head. "Dawn is my best friend and he wouldn't betray me like that."

Serena coughed up some blood into her hand. "Justice, he just broke a couple of my ribs. Why would I lie to you?" Like a child, Justice stormed out of the room. Serena could hear him slam his fist into the table and Aimee begging him to tell her what was wrong.

"It will be okay; he just needs time to process. His best friend just betrayed him. It will be quite raw for a while." Erik wrapped his arm around her waist and pulled her up.

"I hope you're right. Dawn fooled all of us. He said you and Justice have an important destiny. Do you know anything about that?"

Erik shook his head "No, not really. My mother always said that to us. I figured it's what everyone's mom would say. You know—the whole, *you're special, you're going to save the world* spiel."

Serena put a hand on her aching chest. "We need to prepare for what's going to come. We need more accessible weapons, and no one leaves the Sanctuary alone. Is there a way to block off the portals?"

Erik waved his hand in front of the portal. *"Tafnen."* He kissed Serena on the forehead. "No one can come in or out. We need to start our interrogation."

She nodded. "Let's go wake Sleeping Beauty up."

When they walked into the dining room, Gamble was picking up flipped over chairs left from hurricane Justice. "Erik, what happened? Where's Dawn?"

It took a few minutes for Erik to find the right words. His voice was full of betrayal. "Dawn is working for Henrik. He has been sending him notes about what goes on in the Sanctu-ary. He attacked Serena." Gamble sat down.

"Jesus, I am sorry, Erik. I know you have practically raised him since he was ten. We all have your back, and we will finish this."

Erik took a deep breath in and slowly nodded his head. "I know we will finish this, no matter what."

Serena felt her chest rumble as she breathed in. "Listen, I don't want to whine or be a party pooper, but I'm pretty sure I have several broken ribs. Let's try to hurry this up."

Gamble stood in front of Serena. "I can try to take some of the pain away, if you would like? Place my hand on where it hurts the most." Without a thought, she grabbed Gamble's hand, placing it on top of her chest. Gamble mumbled. "*Hele.*" A warm light emerged from his hand. As Serena took a deep breath, the throbbing pain subsided.

"Not to sound ungrateful, but where were you ten minutes ago?"

Gamble patted her shoulder. "I am glad to help any way that I can."

The trio walked down the stairs and stood in front of the robed man's cell. As Gamble unlocked the door, the robed man spat at their feet. "Einherja," his deep voice hissed. In one swift movement, Erik stood in front of the prisoner.

"Now, let's start with something easy. What exactly are you?"

Gamble waved his hand "*Sparke.*" He levitated the ball of fire, slowly inching it closer to the robed man's face. The fire lit up the man's rotting features.

"We are the revenants." The revenant kept his eyes on Serena and smiled, revealing a toothless mouth. "When there is one, there will be many." Serena pulled out her dagger and put it against his throat.

"I will turn you into a pile of goo. He asked what *exactly* you are. We don't know what a revenant is."

"As humans, we were dedicated to evil and sacrificed other humans to Hel. When we died, Hel gave our bodies to her most loyal demons. We will continue to carry out the ritual and raise the knights of Hel. As each sacrifice passes, the veil between the Underworld and Midgard slowly disappears. The blood of a god will complete the ritual. You will not stop this."

Erik puts his hand on the dagger and slowly pushed it deeper into the demon's throat. "What about Henrik? What does he have to do with the ritual?"

The demon shook his head "I don't know what the goddess' plan is for him. She does not tell us everything. Hel is the one and only goddess. All others should bow down to her and beg for their lives."

Serena scoffed. "Please, she isn't that powerful. If she is, why can't she stop that disgusting rot? It makes me gag just thinking about it. *Goddess* and *rotting flesh* do not belong in the same sentence."

The revenant's eyes scowled at Serena. "Blasphemous. Just you wait to see what the goddess has in store for you."

Serena wiggled her fingers. "I am *so* scared; just shaking in my boots."

The revenant frowned, looking down at Serena's feet. "I do not understand. You are not wearing boots."

Serena's mouth dropped. "Wow, that one just blew over your head. Not so smart are you, Mr. Revenant?"

Erik placed a hand on top of her shoulder which edged her to move. "You have had your fun."

Erik locked the cell door. Gamble and Serena looked at each other while they both snickered. Gamble shook his head. "Nothing gets past those revenants."

Erik rolled his eyes. "What can you expect? I bet their brains are all rotted away." Serena jumped up and clapped her hands.

"Good job, Erik. You made a successful joke."

Erik rolled his eyes. "Hey, I make plenty of funny jokes. I don't know what you are talking about."

Gamble covered a snicker with his hand. "Of course, Erik. Whatever you say."

Serena turned towards Gamble. "Just smile and nod. Works every time." She stuck her tongue out at Erik.

Suddenly, something underneath the ground began to move, and the Sanctuary violently shook. Erik grabbed Serena and held onto the cell bars. The sound of glass shattering filled the silence between the large cracking sounds outside. The revenant started to scream.

"You are too late. The ritual will be completed."

# CHAPTER ELEVEN

G AMBLE WAVED A HAND ABOVE THE CREATURE "S TILNE." T HE revenant kept screaming but not a single sound came out of his mouth.

Serena glared at the revenant. "That was annoyingly loud."

The ground slowly stopped moving. Erik rubbed Serena's arm. "We need to gather our weapons and find out where they will be competing the ritual. I don't know if we will be able to defeat the Knights of Hel, but we will try to prevent them from walking on Earth."

Gamble and Serena nodded. They all went back up to dining room. The dark elves scurried around the room, picking up all the broken glass. Justice and Aimee came running in. "What's going on? Did you get any information?" As Erik caught up the couple, Serena snuck off towards the library.

She took out her cellphone and opened her radio app. *"This is Avonmore news, reporting on the gruesome murders found early this morning. Frank Robinson was found dead in front of the public library, and Polly Morrison was also found dead in front of the local high school. Police are currently asking for any clues to either death before the evacuation begins tomorrow at nine am. Due to the 6.5 magnitude earthquake, several gas lines and buildings need extensive repair. Check back on the Avonmore official website to find out when the evacuation order will be lifted. Police are advising all citizens to be cautious."* Serena slammed her fist down on the table.

"What are they doing? Targeting every person that has ever talked to me? They are going to pay for this."

Serena sat down at the table, and began to draw a map of Avonmore. "Mariah was found in her house." She drew a dot on each area where the bodies were found. She connected the dots together. They formed a star with Avonmore Park directly in the middle. "The last sacrifice will be in Avonmore park. This is what Nótt has been preparing for the past two years. This has to be right...

"Erik! Come here. I think I know where the last sacrifice will take place."

The Einherja came running through the door into the library. "Look, if you connect all the murders, it creates an upside-down star. In the middle would be Avonmore Park—that's where the last sacrifice will take place." Erik looked down at her drawing. Serena pointed to the middle of the park. "Of course it has to be a star. They couldn't think of an original shape. In every single damn witch/supernatural movie, there is always an upside-down star."

Aidan slightly raised his hand up. "It's called a pentagram, Serena."

Serena snapped at Aidan. "I know what it's called. I am beyond pissed they have killed four of my friends." Serena held up four fingers. "They have made this personal. I am going to kill them all." Serena slammed her fist down on the table.

"Serena is right. We are going to kill them all." Erik wrapped his arm around Serena's waist. "That is the spirit we need. Right, everyone?"

Aimee nodded. "Definitely going to kill them all. But who are they going to try to sacrifice? They said it needs to be the blood of a god. Aidan and I are safe, but one of you might be targeted." Aimee squeezed Justice's hand.

Erik cleared his throat. "We need to be prepared. They must have a back-up plan if they are unable to grab one of us. The revenant said they are sacrificing all these people to raise the knights of Hel. Let's try to find out as much as we can about them. Aidan and Gamble—you bring out any books you think might be able to help us. I am going to send a message to the Scholars of Vanir to see if they have any idea who they are." Erik left the library to go to his office.

Aidan and Gamble grabbed stacks of books, dividing some to each person. Aimee turned to Serena. "You need to go rest for a while. Even though Gamble did a healing spell, your body still needs time to recuperate."

Serena rubbed her eyes. "Wake me up if you find out anything important." Aimee gave her a slight smile.

Serena wrapped her hand around the bedroom door. *I won't be able to sleep there right now; it just doesn't feel like home.* Instead, she strolled into Erik's room and flopped down on the bed. His signature cinnamon scent radiated off the pillows.

When Serena woke up, she shook violently from the cold. Barefoot, she began to walk across the frozen river. Snow started to blow and surrounded her body. She tried to wrap herself in her arms to warm up. As her vision continued to blur, Serena could make out the outline of someone in the snow. She ran full-speed towards the figure. "Hello? Can you hear me?" Suddenly, all the snow fell to the ground and the wind stopped. Hel materialized right in front of Serena.

"Well look what we have here. Daughter of Nótt, I didn't think we would meet again so soon." Hel reached to touch her face but Serena slapped the hand away. Her hand stung and began to turn black. Hel smirked. "So touchy."

Serena heard a whisper in her ear. *Daughter, use your dagger.* Hel tried to grab her shoulders. She ducked down, and pulled out her gleaming dagger, thrusting it directly into Hel's chest. Black smoke swirled out of the wound and Hel let out a chilling screech.

Serena jerked up. The first thing she saw was Nótt on the edge of the bed, wrapping a blanket around Serena. "You're actually here." Serena hugged the Goddess. "Thank you for taking me out of there."

Nótt pushed the wet hair off Serena's face. "The day of reckoning will be upon you soon. Remember, daughter, I will be there when you need me." Nótt laid Serena back down on the pillow. Serena's eyes shut, and she felt the warmth of Nótt's lips on her forehead. "Sleep, my child."

After what only seemed to be a few minutes, Serena opened her eyes. *Was that also a dream?* She looked down on the bed and saw the same blanket wrapped around her. *She was actually here.* Erik walked through the door towards Serena and kissed her.

"Serena, you are freezing." He rubbed both hands over her goosebumpy arms. He grabbed a thick black wool sweater from the closet and slipped it over her head. "Tell me what happened."

Serena explained what had happened with Hel.

"Your connection with Nótt is deepening. How is your chest?"

Serena took a deep breath in as the achy throb reminded her that it was still there. "It will be fine; I just need to rest a bit longer. Did anyone find out about the Knights of Hel?"

Erik shook his head. "Nothing in any of our books. The scholars have not sent a message back, either." Erik ran his hand through Serena's wet hair.

"Master Erik?" Milia lightly tapped on his bedroom door. "I have some supper for you and Miss Serena." Erik opened the bedroom door. She handed him a tray of lasagna and garlic bread.

"Thank you so much, Milia. I'm starving." A small meow came from behind Milia, and Marbles brooded into the room.

Milia turned towards the tabby and gave him a stern look. "Well, shall we tell them what you did? Naughty kitten." Marbles wrapped his soft tail around Serena's leg. "Mr. Marbles here jumped into a pan of lasagna." Milia waggled her finger towards the tabby. "He almost burnt his paws."

Marbles looked up at Serena with big dopey eyes. "Marbles! Don't jump into hot food! You have to be a good cat and not stress out Milia."

Milia patted Marbles' soft back. "Other than the lasagna incident, he has been a wonderful cat. He has been catching the mice in the garage. He has been following Nathaniel and I into our room at night—we have made him a nice cushion bed."

Serena rubbed Marbles' head. "Good Marbles. You keep Milia and Nathaniel company." As Milia left the room, Marbles followed quickly behind her.

Serena dug her fork into the piece of saucy lasagna. "Silly cat. I'm glad he's keeping Milia and Nathaniel company." Serena took a bite out of the garlic bread. "I can't believe how hungry I am."

Erik froze, watching her eat. He let out a deep chuckle. "You are always hungry. I just don't know where you put it all."

Serena rolled her eyes. *That's because you're not paying attention to how many rolls I have on my stomach.* "Hush, I just love food and coffee. Plus, I just came back from an underworld realm. I deserve a major carb overload."

They sat down on the window nook overlooking the golden fountain as they ate their supper. "Your room has the best view, Erik."

He agreed. "I love it. The sound of the water flowing reminds me of when my mother took Justice and I to go watch the river in Vanir." He got up from the nook and dug through the nightstand drawer, pulling out chocolate peanut butter cups. Unwrapping a piece, he brushed the chocolate across her lips. "Want some?"

She quickly took a bite out of the chocolate. "Can you just stop being so perfect for just one minute?"

He shook his head. "No way. I just want to make you happy." She kissed the top of his head.

"Is this what love truly is? Being corny and feeding each other food? If I had known this, I would have fallen in love sooner."

Erik chuckled while he scooped Serena from off the nook and placed her down onto the bed. He tucked Serena in neatly with a fuzzy blanket. "Get some more rest. I am going to check if there is any progress." Serena started to drift off as she watched Erik leave the room.

§.

The smell of lavender filled the air. Serena bent down to pick up some pink and purple wildflowers. As she raised the flowers to her nose, a sweet little voice yelled out from past the field "Mommy? Where are you?" Serena stood up.

"Over in the wildflowers, Ailsa." The giggly little girl ran through the flowers, followed by a slightly older elf boy. White daisies were pinned all around her long brown curls. Her light violet eyes twinkled as she grabbed Serena's hand.

"Come on, Mommy. We're going to miss Daddy's birthday cake."

The small boy grabbed her other hand. "Hurry, Auntie. We can't miss it." They all ran through the wildflowers, reaching the back of the sanctuary. Erik wore a white linen top and dark jeans and glided towards the trio.

"There are my two favorite girls. You almost missed my cake."

Serena shook her head. "I wasn't very far. Don't worry, I would never miss a chance to eat cake."

Ailsa ran towards the round table, grabbing two pieces of chocolate cake. "Here you go, Mommy." Serena grabbed a spoon off the table and scooped a piece into her mouth.

"That is a *really* delicious cake." Serena smacked her lips together, making chewing noises. Erik chuckled as he rubbed the side of her face.

"Serena." He gently shook her shoulders. "Wake up. You are dreaming. I hate to be the bearer of bad news, but there is no cake." Serena rubbed her mouth as she slowly opened her eyes. "I seem to have to wake you up a lot."

She stretched her arms above her head. "I don't know what to say. I love to sleep. Especially now that my dreams are starting to change and not be so freaky."

He tossed her a bottle of water which she caught and twisted off the lid. Erik studied her face. "You were talking in your sleep about cake." She quickly took a sip of water as her face turned beet red.

"Sorry. I don't know what you are talking about...But I do love cake."

"I have sent word to Vanir, looking for Dawn. There has been no luck. He seems to have disappeared. I am sure my father helped him out. He loves to keep his little spies on a tight leash."

Erik tapped his fingers against the night stand. "What about his family? He told me they have a small farm outside of Vanaheim. He might be hiding with them."

Erik frowned and shook his head. "Dawn has no family. His magic manifested when he was ten years old. He stole a spell book from his older brother. One night, he was practicing a fire spell and it went out of control. Their farmhouse went up in flames. The older brother died saving Dawn. My father was the Elder who took him in after the incident, sending him to the Avonmore Sanctuary."

Serena crossed her arms. "Why would Dawn lie about his family to me?"

Erik shrugged his shoulders. "I guess he probably didn't want you to know Henrik saved him. I am sure my father weaseled the idea into his head that Dawn owed him a life debt. You know, I pretty much raised him. I just wish he could have come to me instead of trusting my father." Putting his hand on top of his heart, Erik tapped. "I have been here for him for the past ten years. I thought that would have meant something to him."

Serena squeezed his shoulders. Erik lowered his head while trying to hide the single tear that rolled down his face. "I have a feeling that Dawn thought if he did this, maybe Justice would love him back and leave Aimee. Justice loves Dawn as much as he does Aimee. Dawn was blind to it, though."

Serena raised her eyebrows.

"I always got the impression he loved Justice as much as a brother...Well, getting back to the reason I woke you up...I would like you to come with me to interrogate the revenant, if you are feeling up to it."

Serena nodded. "Sure. I've been stuck in this room long enough. I just need to change." She grabbed a pair of yoga pants and a t-shirt from a pile of clothes next to the bed. Erik stood watching as Serena slipped off the black wool sweater and toss it into the hamper. He was quieter than usual, his silence hanging over him like a stormy cloud. Serena didn't want to stir the cloud and make him talk about his feelings. Instead, they walked into the library in silence.

Aimee was organizing the weapons on top of a wooden table. Instantly, Justice sat up, watching the couple walk down into the room. "I am coming with you guys this time. I need to do something. Just sitting here is making me stir crazy."

Erik nodded. "Are you sure you are up to it?"

Justice placed a hand on his brother's shoulder "Yes, I am fine. I need to do something other than wait around here."

They continued down into the cells. The revenant wickedly smiled as they entered. "Perfect timing, Einherja." His body began to shake while his eyes turned a deep blood red.

"Hello, Serena." Hel's voice sent chills down her spine. "And the sons of Baldr. You're both almost as beautiful as he was."

The revenant seductively licked its rotting lips. "The son of Dellinger, or, as you call him, Dawn, is being prepared as the final sacrifice. Come and try to save him, little Einherja." Hel howled into the air like werewolf, erupting a yellow Sulphur cloud. The prisoner disappeared into a black puddle.

Justice jolted up the stairs, followed by Erik. "Justice! You can't go. It is a trap. They want us to get emotional and make a mistake!"

Nothing Erik said stopped him; he was on the war path.

Finally, Justice stopped in the library and wrapped a leather sheath over his shoulder, filling it with a long silver sword. Then, he wrapped a belt sheath around his waist. Justice took a deep breath in before he turned to Erik. "I have to go; I know he betrayed us, but Dawn still is my best friend. He is sacrificing himself to protect me. I need to try to protect him."

Aimee secured a sheath belt around her waist. "If you are going, I am going. There is no way I am letting you go alone."

Serena pushed Aimee's hand away and took the belt off. "Aimee, you can't—the baby. I'll go. Gamble and Aidan, will you stay with Aimee in case they find a way to attack the Sanctuary?"

They both nodded. In no time at all, Erik had slipped his

gear on. It was if he had memorized which part went where. "All right, well, I can't let my baby brother and my girl go alone. We need to make a plan before we reach the park. Let's head out and be careful, everyone. Aimee, you are in charge while I am gone."

Aimee gave Erik a quick nod, before grabbing Justice and kissing him firmly on the lips. "Please, be safe. I love you. Promise me you will come home." He bent down and kissed Aimee's stomach, then kissed her one last time on the lips.

"I will. I love you both so much."

Aimee wrapped both arms tightly around Serena, it felt as though she didn't want to let go. "Please be careful, and bring him back to us."

Serena rubbed her friend's trembling arms which seemed to soothe them a bit.

"I'll do what I can."

# CHAPTER TWELVE

THE SILENCE WAS THICK WHILE THE TRIO DROVE DOWN TO Avonmore. Both Serena's legs shook uncontrollably and her stomach felt queasy. *It's going to be okay. We just need to get this over with, Aimee will have the baby, and it will be happily ever after.*

The ride ended at the closet cul-de-sac. The neighbourhood looked abandoned. The silence was eerie; Serena was used to the noise of children running down the street, and of radios blaring. Avonmore looked and felt as if it was stuck in a horror movie, waiting for the bad guys to pop out.

Serena smoothed the drawn map over the top of the car. "There are four ways into the park. We shouldn't all attack in the same direction. I'll enter the south entrance. Justice, come from the east, and Erik, you come from the north. In my dream, the sacrifice was taking place just off the main dirt path in the pine trees. Once you reach the main path, you will be able to take any side path—they all lead to the center of the trees."

Justice nodded "If either of you get overwhelmed, shoot a bright white light into the air."

While he whipped his hand in the air, Justice said *"Tenne."*

A bright white light shot into the sky, and fragmented into tiny sparkles. "Try it out, Serena. Just try to imagine a bright light shooting out of your hand."

She slowly waved her hand and whispered, *"Tenne."* A small bright light sputtered from out of her hand. *Whoa! I can't believe I did that on my first try. Badass Barista learns magic!*

Justice patted Serena on the shoulder. "Good first try. Be safe, both of you, and let's kick these demon butts back to Hel."

Erik pulled Justice in for a hug. "Let's end this, brother. May Odin give us battle wisdom and strength of strategy. Hail Odin."

Justice lowered his head. "Hail Odin."

Serena looked up into the sky. "Hail Odin." *Please protect us.*

In silence, Erik and Serena watched as Justice disappeared into the night. Erik grabbed onto her shoulders, pulling her into a kiss. He wrapped both hands around her waist. "I love you, no matter what happens."

Serena could feel the tears brewing. She bit down onto her lip. "Always and forever." Holding hands as they walk towards the park, Serena kissed Erik's lips one last time before he vanished into the darkness. *Please be safe, Erik.*

Serena shook both arms and took a deep breath in. "All right! I can do this. This is what you've been training for. It's time to end this mess." Her body still trembled as she walked down the rocky road, turning to take the side path through the dark pine trees. *This is the moment of truth.* As she reached the center, nothing was disturbed. There was no sign of Dawn, no rocks shaped like pentagrams.

*Silly barista — it's a trap. Remember what you've been dreaming about for the past two years.* The sound of crunching leaves came from behind her. *My spider senses are tingling.* Pulling out the daggers, she lifted them just in front of her shoulders. She jabbed the left dagger quickly behind her, into the

Adam's apple of one the revenants. *Got you. One down, and who knows how many more to go?* Slightly lunging, Serena thrust Natt into the next revenant's fleshy knee cap. *Two down.* She whipped around, but a fist hit the side of her face. In a daze, she stumbled back. Two pairs of cold hands grabbed hold of her arms. She lashed her left arm as hard as she could, unlocking the grip of one. Using her free arm, she turned and scratched the face of the revenant next to her.

Two more crept out of the pine trees, jolting towards Serena. She slowly backed away from the attackers. *Where the hell are Justice and Erik?* She tripped over a rock and landed on her wrist. *Shit.* The revenants circled around her like hyenas going for their prey.

Simultaneously, each pulled out a dagger. Serena wasn't sure which one let out a cackle. "The Goddess will be pleased."

She swiftly waved her hand into the air. "*Tenne.*" The bright white light flickered for a moment and then shot into the sky. Justice ran out of the pine trees, his face drenched in blood and black goo.

He waved a hand towards the circling attackers. "*Sparke.*"

The first revenant lit on fire quickly, like a dry bush; the whole circle was engulfed in flames. Justice waved his hand again. "*Vann.*" A wave of water doused the flames. The revenants' sizzling bones fell to the ground and liquefied. He offered Serena his hand and pulled her up. "Where is Erik?"

Serena shook her head. "I don't know. We need to hurry and find him."

Serena and Justice bolted off into the dark pine trees. As they reached the edge of the park, Erik's body was splayed on the ground, surrounded by revenants. *Is he moving? I can't tell.*

"Get away from him, you freaks!" Serena screamed, running full throttle towards the circle. She jumped onto the back of one revenant, stabbing him in the side of his throat. Another pulled her off and tried to kick her in the stomach.

She quickly grabbed his leg, shoving him backwards into a metal pole.

Justice yelled, *"Amar,"* sending a boulder flying into the air, crushing the last revenant.

Serena rushed towards Erik. "Erik, wake up! Please Odin, don't let him die." She dragged him out of the dirt penta-gram, onto the grass, and lightly tapped his face. *Please be alive.* Serena placed her head on his chest; a faint thumping tickled her ear. *Oh, thank you. Thank the gods!*

For what seemed like a few minutes, Serena lay motion-less and unaware of the situation. Justice yelled "Serena!". She snapped out of the trance. He was surrounded by five revenants. "Behind you!" *Smack.* A hard, blunt object hit the back of her head. Crumpling down onto the ground, her vision became blurred. A heavy foot slammed down onto her back. She tried to get up, but the heel of the foot dug itself deeper into her back. Stomping down on her back again, Serena felt her newly healed bones crack and the familiar throbbing flared up. She began to cough uncontrollably. Justice whipped his sword towards the attackers, trying to push them back.

The two revenants behind him grabbed onto his arms, pulling him down onto the pentagram. As he continued to struggle, one kicked him in the stomach. The circle of attackers pulled out daggers from their robes. Unsuccessfully, Justice tried bucking his body. The revenant kept a steady hand on top, pushing Justice harder down into the ground. "Your sacrifice will not be in vain, Son of Baldr." One by one, each revenant took turns carving into his skin.

Serena had never seen so much blood.

Each wound spewed out more, creating a small bloody river on top of the gravel. Justice let out one last howl as his struggling body slowed down. Burning tears rolled down Serena's face. *Please Erik, wake up.*

Serena tried to cover her ears as a blood curdling shriek

filled the air. Aimee ran towards the revenants, quickly lifting both of her hands high up in the air and gasping. "*Kvele*," she screamed as the revenants grabbed onto their throats and panted for air. Their faces turned a deep blue as they all fell to the ground, sulphur seeping out of their bodies.

"Justice...please be alive." She kneeled next to his limp body, pulling him up into her arms. "I can't do this without you. Please don't leave me." Tears rolled down her face as she lay him back down on the ground. "Please, I need you." Aimee began pumping both hands on top of his chest. Tilting his head back, she pinched his nose and blew directly into his mouth. "No. Wake up. Odin, you can't let him go like this. He is not ready for Valhalla." Aimee swished her hand above his body. "*Cuil*."

Gamble ran up behind Aimee, grabbing her hand. "Stop it, Aimee. He is gone. Don't try to resurrect him; he wouldn't want that, and whatever came back wouldn't be Justice. You need to think of the consequences."

In the corner of Serena's eye, she watched Aidan beside Erik, feeling around his wrist. "Erik is okay! I found a pulse. Gamble, help me with him."

Every inch Serena pushed off the ground, each bone screamed in agony. Gamble wrapped both hands around Erik's shoulder, shaking him. "Erik, we need you. Get up!" Finally up on two feet, Serena dragged her limp legs to Aimee. That was as far as she could go. Both knees buckled, and she slammed down into the gravel.

Serena's voice cracked. "He saved both our lives. Justice was so strong and brave." The continuous tears fell down Aimee's face, and her breath was short and coarse.

With both arms wrapped around Justice's back, she began to rock him back and forth. "I'm so sorry. I should have come."

A thundering boom arose from below. The ground started to viciously tremor, causing ripples to break open the very earth. Aimee pulled Justice off the gravel, placing him on the grass. Aidan hooked his two arms around Serena's shoulders, pulling her towards the grass. Serena army crawled towards Erik, and flopped down next to him. The ripples spread quickly across the gravel, with geysers of water and steam shooting out. Drops of sweat trickled down Serena's spine. Steam sizzled up from the shoots of grass. The ruptures began cracking the grass. Serena watched gravel crumble, disappearing into the holes.

Gamble shouted, "We need to get out of here!"

Both boys wrapped Erik's arms around their shoulders, heading towards the cul-de-sac. Without any effort, as if she were Superwoman, Aimee hoisted Justice over her shoulder.

"We will be back for you, Serena. I promise you." She nodded, watching her friend disappear into the trees. The sweat blurred her vision. Serena tried to wipe it off, but it continued to pour down. *I am not going to die here. Get up, Serena.*

The smoke in the air became thick and suffocating. Serena gasped, her breathing heavy and jagged. She felt as if she were stuck in a sauna. Creaks and groans filled the air as the pine trees fell into the cracks, instantly lighting on fire. Enormous stone spikes punctured through the earth, pulling out a stone staircase.

With much effort, Serena dragged her body behind a big rock. One by one, getting louder each time, piercing trotters came up the staircase. She peeked around the rock. On top of the emerged staircase stood four horses. The skin on each horse was hanging off, revealing bone and blood. Their piercing red eyes shifted around the park. Black smoke came out of the horses' nostrils as they let out a bloodcurdling neighs. She could feel something warm dripping out of her ears and wiped at the liquid. Looking down at her hands, she saw blood smeared over her fingers. *What the hell?* She slapped both hands on top of her ears and glanced around the rock. On each horse sat a skeleton rider. Unlike the horses, the flesh was completely missing, but somehow, they still had clothes strapped on their boney bodies. *How is this even possible? Skeletons? Zombie horses?* The skeleton nearest to Serena had deep red glowing eyes, and was carrying a large silver scythe. The two skeleton warriors in the middle held twin metal swords. The final skeleton had a quiver and bow strapped to its bony back. He pulled the horse into the forest. Each branch that grazed the rider began to light on fire. He disappeared deep into the trees, ash trailing.

*Knights of Hel! What am I going to do?* A broken branch crunched behind her. She turned to see the trio of Einherja coming out of the bushes. She quickly pointed down to the ground and they slowly ducked. One knight lifted his sword, pointing towards the trees. His voice hissed, *"Det høres ut!"* Two skeletons trotted towards the pine trees. As they passed the rock, Serena could feel the burning breath of the undead horses.

Aimee and the boys quickly got back up, running the way they came towards the cul-de-sac. "Einherja!" the skeleton screeched. The knight raised its flaming sword, slashing down the pine trees. The branches quickly dissipated into ash. *I can't let them reach the others. I need to distract them.* Serena quietly crawled to the other side of the burning rock. *Please, Nótt, protect me. I'm going to do something very stupid.* The moment Serena was going to step out from behind the rock, a warm tingling moved through her body. Nótt's soothing voice entered her head. *I told you I would protect you, daughter.*

Serena felt as if she were shoved into the darkest corner of her body. She tried to scream but not a single peep came out. As if it were a dream and she was a passenger, Serena watched Nótt levitate her into the air. Her long brown hair transformed into a majestic silver color. Looking down at her hands, her skin looked painted by the deepest black. Nótt's enchanting voice spoke through her. "Knights of Hel, you don't belong on this realm. Leave now or perish." Nótt pulled out the dagger and ran her hand over the top of the blade. It transformed into a sword. The knights charged towards her. She grabbed onto the skeleton with the flaming sword, lifted him up into the air and threw him down the stone stairs. Nótt waved her hand above the horses and whispered, "*Sove.*" Without a sound, each horse fell to the ground, turning into a pile of ash. The next knight swung his sword towards Serena. Quickly, she blocked it with Natt, knocking the sword out of his hand. She kicked his knee out of his bony leg, turning it into a pile of dust. He screamed, and she raised her sword, beheading the knight.

The scythe-wielding knight crept up behind Serena. He lifted the silver curved blade, slashing it across her back. *Shit.* Serena whimpered. Like a ghost, Nótt disappeared into the night, materializing behind him. She waved a hand over the attacker. "*Aske.*" The knight instantly crumbled into ash. A cluster of arrows came whizzing through the air towards Nótt. She lifted her hand up. "*Sakte Ned.*" The arrows stopped, as if they were frozen in time. As Nótt twirled her finger around, the arrows mimicked the direction. "*Forover.*" The arrows sped towards the knight, landing in the center of his skull. Like the others, the knight turned to ash.

Hel strolled up the stone stairs, clapping. "Well done, Nótt. You destroyed my knights. But now, the veil between the realms is at its weakest. You know what that means: thousands of my followers will be able to roam the earth. There is no way Serena will be able to kill them all."

Nótt raised her hands. "*Sparke.*" A cluster of fireballs flew towards Hel.

Hel smirked and whispered, "*Reflektere.*" The balls turned around and rushed backwards. Nótt dodged them, disappearing into the night, and popping back up behind Hel.

"You think your little parlor tricks will work on me?" Nótt

lifted Natt into the air, slashing down into Hel's shoulder. Hel pulled out the sword. With one swift flick, she threw Nótt into the air. Serena's body slammed down into a flaming pine tree. "And your miserable little sword?"

"Serena, where are you?" She could hear Erik's voice echo through the forest. He rushed through, with Aidan and Gamble trailing close behind him. "Serena! Please answer me." Each boy froze in fear. Hel chuckled wildly, winking at the boys.

"Well, look who it is. I will see you all very soon. I can promise you that." She vanished into the night. The fire continued spreading throughout the trees.

"Erik, if we don't do something, this fire will burn Avonmore down."

Erik nodded. "Everyone hold hands." The Einherja held each other's hands, yelling, "*Vann.*" A huge wave of blue water appeared, dousing the park.

The tingle slowly dissipated and Serena could feel Nótt slipping away. *My daughter. One day we will stop Hel; I can promise you that. The gods will never forgive such treachery.*

Serena could barely open her eyes, gasping for air. Her lungs felt on fire, and she coughed up water. She imagined this is what drowning felt like. Her teeth clanked and shivered. She tried to call for Erik, but the words failed to come out.

The boys dashed towards Serena. "Serena, are you okay? Erik pulled off his sweater, slipping it over Serena's head. "What happened to you? A piece of your hair is a different color." He pulled the strip of hair out of the wet mess, the usual brown shimmering silver.

Her voice was strained. "Nótt...saved me."

Erik squeezed Serena, kissing the top of her head. "We will have to say a blessing to Nótt. I don't know what I would do if I lost you too." *Too?*

Serena's body began to shake; she almost had forgotten

about Justice. It was hard for her to come up with the words. Erik must have seen the confusion on her face; he shook his head and tears rolled down his cheeks. "He was incredible. Justice saved both our lives. I would be dead if it wasn't for him."

Erik grabbed both of her hands, pulling Serena up onto her feet. Serena stumbled as she tried to walk. "Home...I just want to go home."

"We will go right away," Erik agreed. "There is a lot that I need to do."

Serena frowned. "What do you mean?" *Did you actually just say that? What is wrong with you? His brother just died. He needs a funeral.* "Sorry, Erik. I didn't mean for that to come out the way it did."

His normally relaxed demeanor tensed as his eyes drifted away. "I know. We are all still processing his death." His tone of voice was unreadable and cold. Serena shook her head. *Way to put your foot in your mouth. Good job, Serena.*

# CHAPTER THIRTEEN

"WE HAVE SEVEN DAYS UNTIL JUSTICE'S SOUL CAN ENTER Valhalla. I need to prepare his funeral and build his pyre." A crackle shot through Erik's voice, his words strained. "I still can't believe he's gone. My best friend…the only family I have left…" The closer they got to the car, Erik's grip grew tighter. Aimee sat in the backseat, wrapped around Justice's body. *Oh, Aimee. If only I could turn back and save him, like he saved me.* Aimee looked up at Serena, her face blotchy. Serena offered a hand towards Aimee, and her shaky hand grasped Serena's.

Aidan came up to the car. "Gamble and I are going to try to block off this crevice. We don't want anyone wandering into the park. We will just walk home."

Erik turned towards the young elf. "That is a good idea. Just be careful. If you run into any trouble, come home right away." Aidan nodded and waved as Erik drove off. Serena watched the boy rush back into the forest

"I can drive back, if you would like."

Erik shook his head. "I need the distraction right now."

The car ride back to the Sanctuary was quiet, except for the occasional soft whimpers coming from Aimee. Every so often, Serena turned to check on her. *Now what? Justice is dead, and Hel's minions will be on the loose soon—or so she says.* She opened the mirror on the sun visor, caressing the shimmering silver streak in her hair. *Nótt, what are we going to do now? How will we stop her? How would you even stop a god?* As they returned to the Sanctuary, Erik parked the car beside the water fountain. Both dark elves were waiting outside, fully dressed in black. Nathaniel helped Erik carry Justice inside as Milia wrapped her arms around a sobbing Aimee. *I need to get some rest. Tonight was too much.* Serena's body strained the entire way up to her room. Lifting off her blood-soaked t-shirt, she threw it down onto the ground. *I need to make my skin feel numb.*

She walked into the bathroom and twisted the hot tap. Letting the steam fill the room, she slipped off her ripped yoga pants. When she entered the hot shower, which made her head become woozy, Serena couldn't help but to hunch over. Her stomach twisted and turned and whatever contents in there made their way back up.

*He is dead. It's all my fault. I couldn't save Justice. Erik will hate me forever.* After the hot water became cool, Serena wrapped the fuzziest purple towel around her body. She studied the footprint bruise on her back. After grabbing a comb, she roughly brushed the knots out of her hair. *I should have died. At least Erik would still have a brother, and the baby would have a father.* Tightness began on the left side of her temple. Her stomach became queasy as a chill rushed over through her body. Serena pulled out a black set of silk pajamas, slipping them over the goosebumps. The tightness turned into a pounding rhythm. Serena's body gave way and she collapsed down onto the soft bed.

During her sleep, a continuous loop of Justice's death played over in her head. She finally sat up and screamed, "Enough!" A rancid smell climbed up into Serena's nose.

Looking around the room, on top of her nightstand sat sour yogurt and browned apple slices. *How long have I been asleep?*

A loud crunch and thump came from outside her window. She walked towards it and sat down in the nook. Erik and Nathaniel took turns chopping down the surrounding trees in perfect rhythm. Gamble and Aidan were piling the logs into a huge stack. Over and over, Serena watched the men work. Not a single word was said, nor a single break taken.

Milia strolled into the room, carrying a tray of fruit. She startled as she noticed Serena staring out the window. "Pardon me, Miss Serena. I did not think you would be awake yet." Serena walked toward the elderly elf, grabbing the tray of fruit from her frail hands.

"That's okay, Milia. How long have I been asleep?"

Milia cleared the rancid food. "A couple of days. Erik told everyone not to disturb you. You have been through a great deal."

Serena slightly smiled. "Thank you. How is he doing?" Milia walked towards the window, looking down at all the men working.

"Not well, miss. He isn't sleeping. He just continues to gather the wood for the funeral. I expect they will be done for tomorrow morning." Serena held the door open while Milia took the tray and dirty clothes, and shuffled quickly down the hallway. Her stomach rumbled loudly. She sunk her teeth into a juicy peach as she watched Erik slam his axe into the log. *I can't even imagine the pain he is going through right now—how raw it still is.* She threw on a pair of black sweatpants and Erik's grey baggy sweater.

Serena carried the half-eaten tray of fruit down into the kitchen and found a pot of lukewarm coffee. *Good enough.*

After pouring herself several cups of coffee, Serena left the house and walked to where she had seen Erik chopping the trees. At this point, everyone sat around the backyard, wiping the sweat off their heads and silently enjoying some treats that Milia had brought out.

She grabbed a log and placed it on top of the flat wooden base. Lifting the axe, Serena slammed it down as hard as she could, splitting the log in half. *My dad would be so proud of me.* With every log split, the base became overwhelmed. She gathered the logs and placed them on top of the stack. Erik opened his hand towards Serena. "Thank you." His words were cool and uninviting. Nodding, she placed the axe handle in his hands and backed away.

Serena whispered in a soft voice, "You're welcome."

The sun began to set. The sky was painted in a collection of pinks, oranges and yellows. The fluffy white clouds disappeared. Milia walked back and forth from the edge of the forest. In her hand, she held a wooden basket. She plucked flowers of every color and green sprigs of trees. Milia motioned for Serena. "We will place these flowers on the pyre. The fire will appease Odin and he will welcome Justice into Valhalla. Danu will accept the flowers as a sacrifice and bless Justice's journey to the next life."

Serena helped Milia spread the flowers across the base of the stack. Milia placed a hand on top of the pile and closed her eyes. "Danu, mother of all, bless this journey." Before Serena placed the wild lavender down, she brushed the flower against her nose. Closing both eyes, a picture of Ailsa flashed in her mind, followed by the sweet little voice calling her 'Mommy'.

*Could it actually be true? This future? Can there be happiness when Erik has already lost so much?* The men cleaned up the area, placing the tools away. Aidan and Gamble scrambled around, picking up the small pieces of wood scattered across the yard. Milia wrapped her arm around Serena and gave her a little squeeze. "Miss Serena, it's best to go to sleep. We have done all we can. The funeral will be tomorrow morning."

She nodded, watching Erik go back inside. *Maybe he is*

*ready to talk.* Serena followed him inside, but he never turned back once, going straight into his room.

Serena went into her room and headed for the closet. She pulled out a black dress and lay it out for the morning. Soft scratching, followed by a loud meow, came from the hallway. Serena pulled open the bedroom door. Marbles ran in, wrapping his fuzzy tail around her leg.

"Marbles where have you been, silly cat? I hope you haven't caused too many problems for Milia." She sprawled out on the bed, Marbles snuggling deep between her arm. "I just don't know how Erik will ever forgive me." Her nose began to sniffle and tears fell down her cheeks. Marbles purred, rubbing his fluffy cheek against her arm. Letting herself drift away, she closed her eyes and prayed to the gods not to repeat Justice's death.

Serena woke up in the backyard of the Sanctuary. Justice's body was woven like a cocoon on top of the stack of logs. Nótt wandered around the wooden pyre, hovering deep blue flames above her hands. She lowered both hands on top of the lifeless body. Each time, both flames burnt out. Shaking her head, the goddess turned towards Serena.

"Hel has his soul; he will not enter Valhalla. The Valkyries will not let him pass. He will spend eternity in the underworld. Daughter, you need to wake up. Hel will be here soon."

# CHAPTER FOURTEEN

Unravelling the blanket and gently pushing Marbles to the side, Serena stretched both arms out. *Why would Hel need Justice's soul? Hasn't she done enough damage?* She slipped on the black dress and flats. Serena peeked down into the back-yard. Everything was already set up for the funeral. She swallowed a gulp of air. *Poor Justice. He never deserved to die like this.*

She crouched down underneath the bed, pulling out two leather thigh sheaths. Serena slipped both daggers in. Buckling the sheathes around her thighs, she quickly peeked into the mirror one last time. *Armed and ready for everything to go wrong.*

Serena made her way to Aimee's room. She softly knocked. "Aimee, it's Serena. Can I come in?" Serena leaned against the door, only to hear sobbing. While she pushed open the door, Aimee sat on the bed, surrounded by men's clothing. In her hand, she had a white tunic, and ran it across her cheek. *The wedding tunic.* Serena ran a hand down the side of the elf's tear-soaked cheek.

"Oh Aimee, I'm going to help get you ready to say goodbye to him."

Aimee squeezed the tunic, forming it into a ball. "I can't do this without him. I can't live without him. I can't raise this baby by myself."

Serena pulled the tunic out of her hands, wrapping one hand around Aimee's. "I promised Justice I would protect you and this baby with my life. I promise I will never leave you. Erik and I will help you. We will not let you raise the baby alone. You will never be alone."

"It's just not the same. I am so scared to be without him."

Serena rubbed circles around Aimee's back. "I understand, but you are a strong woman. It's okay to be scared. I will always help you. So, let me help you get ready?" Aimee weakly nodded.

For a few minutes, Serena flipped through the closet, pulling out the flowy white wedding dress. "Justice would want you to wear this. You looked so beautiful on your wedding day. I think he would like to see it one last time."

Aimee slipped the dress on. "Justice and I once watched this program about medieval funerals and how royalty would wear white. I thought it was beautiful."

Serena braided Aimee's hair, letting some curly pieces frame her face. "I think I would want everyone to wear something fun to my funeral. Maybe superhero costumes or rainbow outfits."

A sad smile crossed Aimee's face. The elf let out a huge breath while grabbing a hold of Serena's arm. "Let's go. I'm ready. I just want to get this over with."

Serena nodded. *Me too.* As they walked out of the room, Milia hurried up the stairs with a basket full of flowers wrapped around her arms. "Oh, Miss Aimee, you look very lovely."

Serena grabbed a handful of bluish purple flowers, gently placing them into Aimee's braid. "These are beautiful." When Serena turned to Milia, the dark elf wiped away the tears rolling down her smokey grey cheeks.

"Yes. Periwinkle. Many place them on alters to Odin."

Milia held onto Aimee's free arm and the trio headed towards the funeral. *Here goes...* As they began to get closer to the backyard, Serena could feel her friend's arms begin to tremor.

"It's going to be okay." The moment they walked into the backyard, Aimee's body buckled. She tried to hold back the tears. Serena pulled Aimee back onto her feet. Erik, who stood at the foot of the pyre, took one step towards them. Serena locked her eyes with his and shook her head. His wispy black hair was slicked back, and was dressed head to toe in black.

Nathaniel and the boys sat in the front row with Marbles. Milia squeezed Aimee's arm and gave her a kiss on the cheek. "Danu will protect him and Odin will open his arms wide for Justice." Aimee stood for a moment, staring at the pyre without even blinking.

"I am ready." Serena helped Aimee onto a wooden chair, without letting go of her crushing grip.

Erik's eyes locked with Serena's, giving one swift nod. Serena wanted to run up and hold him as tight as she could. *I am here for you.* She held both of Aimee's hands as Erik began to speak.

"My baby brother was a great man." His voice cracked. "He lived and died in the service of Odin. The Valkyries will open their arms wide to accept such a gallant warrior. He will remain with our mother, Ailsa, until the day he is chosen to be reborn. Until we meet again, brother."

Everyone lowered their heads and repeated after Erik. "Until we meet again."

Aimee grabbed a handful of flowers, scattering them across the body, and blew him one last kiss. "Until we meet again, my love. May you wait for me in the halls of Valhalla." She sat back down weeping, snuggling her face into Serena's shoulder. Serena tried to bite down to hold off the tears, but they flowed anyway.

Erik lifted both of his hands *"Sparke."* Two deep blue flames appeared. He bent down, placing the flames on top of Justice. As the flame hit the cloth, it instantly snuffed out. Once again, Erik placed his hands down on top of his brother. Both eyebrows furrowed; he moved to the other side of the wooden stack.

"What is going on?" Aimee's face scowled. She walked towards Justice and tried to light the logs on fire. Like before the flames died out. Erik whispered into Aimee's ear; she shook her head and shrugged.

Loud clapping thundered behind all of them.

"What a beautiful service," Nina snickered. She held on tightly onto Henrik's arm as they walked through the door. Aimee whipped around.

"What the hell are you two doing here?"

Nina's face scrunched up. "Excuse me? I was supposed to marry Justice. Maybe if he'd married me, he wouldn't have died."

Aimee lifted both her hands. *"Amar."* A huge boulder whistled towards Nina and Henrik. "You shut your mouth," she screamed.

A half-smile was painted across his face when Henrik stepped to the side. "You really need to do better than that. I thought you were supposed to be a talented sorcerer."

Aimee repeated the spell but louder this time.

Hel appeared in front of Nina, waving her hand *"Forsvinne."* The boulder exploded into tiny pieces and fell to the ground. "Now, that is no way to treat my daughter, Nyx." With a crooked smile on her face, Nina waved a hand above her face. *"Doltha."* Her blonde hair transformed into long black hair, and her blue eyes turned a deep blood red. *I knew something was wrong with her.* Nyx quickly shot Serena a nasty look, as if she could read her thoughts. Erik stood still in front of Justice with his eyes locked onto his fathers.

"What are you doing here? Haven't you done enough?"

Hel ran a hand across the edges of the logs. "Well, Erik, it seems like you have a big problem. I have Justice's soul, and he won't be able to enter Valhalla without it. I will see to it that his precious soul will be tortured for all eternity." In one swift step, Aimee stood behind Hel.

"You rotten witch." Lifting her hands up in the air, she screamed, "*Sparke*." Flames engulfed Hel's entire body. Without even a bother, Hel stepped closer to Erik and shook them off like they were droplets of water.

"That was really rude, little elf. I was talking to Erik."

Hel clenched her fist towards Aimee. "*Kvele*." Aimee fell to the ground, grasping at her neck.

Erik grabbed Hel's arm. "Stop this!"

She shook her head. "No. Not until you all know who is in charge now." Hel placed a hand on top of Aimee's stomach. She turned towards Nyx and shook her head. "I see the elf blood is strong, but not what I am looking for. It's your lucky day." Aimee curled herself into a ball.

Nyx let out a heinous laugh, keeping her eyes glued on Aimee. "So pathetic that Justice picked a sniffling coward over me."

Serena jumped out of the seat, pulling Natt out from the leather sheath. She ran her hand along the blade, transforming it into a sword. A surge of adrenaline raced around her body, she leapt towards Hel, thrusting the sword directly into Hel's heart. Hel whispered into Serena's ear. "It will take a lot more than that to kill me, half-breed."

Without even flinching, Hel slowly pulled out the blade from her chest. Serena pulled out the other dagger, jabbing it quickly into Hel's side. "Don't worry. Someday, I will find a way to kill you. It might not be tomorrow, or next year, or in ten years. Just know—I will kill you eventually."

Hel pulled out the dagger and slapped Serena in the face with the hilt. "You just won't give up, will you? Foolish girl." She threw the dagger into the field and balled her hand up. "*Kvele.*"

Serena fell to her knees, grasping her throat. Each breath became harder than the last. *Is this how I'm going to die?* Hel placed a hand against Serena's stomach. Hel clapped like a small child, her face giddy with glee. "Very good. Empty."

Serena flinched back. Nyx jumped up and clapped her hands. "This is so exciting. I love it when the plan works out accordingly." Hel strolled back to Erik and placed a hand on top of his shoulder. His face scrunched in disgust. In the corner of her eye, Serena could see Aidan and Gamble slowly moving towards Hel. She whipped around, waggling her finger towards the boys.

"Let's not do something we will regret. You boys turn around, and I will forget all about the sneakiness."

Neither said a word, immediately backing down to their seats. "Now, before I get interrupted again, I will give you back Justice's soul if you do me one tiny little favor. Plus, I won't kill the half-breed or the pregnant elf."

Erik stared blankly out into space, Serena tried to catch a glimpse of his eye with no luck. "Fine; what other choice do I have? I'll do whatever you want. Just let them go."

Henrik smiled "Good boy. Such a quick learner." Erik shot a nasty look towards his father. *If only looks could kill...I bet Henrik would have died a thousand times over.*

With a flick of her wrist, Hel lit the stack of logs on fire. She released her grasp. Both girls let out a loud gasp, clenching their throats. Serena coughed and winced, trying to get as much air as she possibility could back into her lungs. *What does she want from Erik?* No one spoke a word until Justice and the logs were entirely turned to ash. "The Valkyries will open their arms wide for you, little brother. Go on forth to the halls of Valhalla where the brave shall live forever. I love you." A warm gust lifted the ashes, and the small grey clouds danced through the pale blue sky. For just a moment, Serena would swear that she could see the clouds welcoming Justice with open arms. *The Valkyries.*

Aimee's eyes were glued to the sky, Serena helped Aimee back into her seat. "Are you okay?" Aimee nodded, then shot a dark glare at Hel. Serena launched herself to Erik, lacing her fingers in between his. *Whatever she wants, we can handle it. I will help him.*

Hel looked Serena up and down, her pointy nose scrunched in the air, "How bittersweet. Would you like to know what you agree to?" Erik's eyes went wide and he squeezed Serena's hand tightly. She didn't want him to let go of her ever.

"What could you possibly want from me? You already took my brother."

Hel motioned for Nyx to come to her. "You are going to marry my daughter. She will help you run this Sanctuary, and in time, you will give me a grandchild."

Serena's face darkened and she protested. "You don't have to do this; we will find a way to stop her."

Erik instantly dropped her hand. Serena followed his gaze to his mother's ring. With one swift motion, he pulled it off her finger. Serena sniffled and her body began to shake.

"Please don't do this."

Hel continued to laugh. "Sad little half-breed. No one has the power to stop me. Not you, and definitely not Nótt." Hel's ember eyes stayed glued on Serena's face "I will have a seat on the council, which is my birth right. Henrik will be my representative with the Elders, as I continue to the rule the underworld." She ran a finger with a painted black nail down Erik's face. "So, Erik, you will make my daughter happy, or I will kill the rest of the people you love."

Hel snapped her fingers and disappeared. Even though

she was gone, Serena could hear her laugh echo through the backyard.

Avoiding any eye contact with Serena, Erik jerked away. Tears rolled down her face as she tried to grab his arm. "Please, Erik, we can fight this. I love you. Always and forever. Don't do this."

Erik shook his head. "Just stop already." He walked towards Nyx and kneeled in front of her. "Would you do me the honor of becoming my wife?"

Nyx jumped up. She snatched the ring out of Erik's palm and shoved it on her pale finger. "I would love to. And don't worry, Serena, you're not invited to our wedding."

*Like I'm going to just sit back and let him marry some demon slut.*

Henrik patted Erik on the shoulder. "This is a good decision, son; this will be a powerful union for our family. Nyx is from a pure lineage: no human or elf blood."

Aimee darted out of her chair, rushing towards Erik. "Please, Erik, don't do this. They killed your brother. Henrik helped. Justice would want you to fight."

"Nyx is right. Maybe if Justice hadn't fallen in love with you, he would have been alive," he snapped.

Aimee put her hand on her heart. "How can you say that to me?"

Nyx hooked her arm around Erik's and pushed Aimee down into the dirt. "You are all so pathetic. You really should stop embarrassing yourselves."

Serena rushed over, looping her hands underneath Aimee hoisting her up off the ground. She swiped the dirt from the white dress and spat in Nyx's direction. "If you ever touch her again, I will kill you."

Nyx let out her signature annoying laugh. "Is that so? Well, I am not very scared, now that I have a handsome fiancé. He won't let anything happen to me, will you?"

Erik shook his head "Of course not." Serena crossed her

arms and tried to hold in her snicker but ended up bursting out laughing.

"I almost feel bad for you, Nyx. You have to get your mother to blackmail a man to marry you. How sad to be married to someone who loves *me*."

Nyx wrapped a finger around Erik's chin and turned his face in for a sloppy kiss. *Ugh!* Erik cleared his throat.

"I don't love you. You and Aimee are the reason my brother is dead. You both need to pack your things and leave immediately. You are not welcome here anymore." *What?* Erik's voice was emotionless and his eyes looked defeated.

"You can't do this, Erik." Aimee protested. Hand in hand, Erik and Nyx walked towards the house.

Without looking back, his voice growled, "If you do not leave in the next hour, I will have no choice but to send you both to Fengsel." Henrik followed the couple back into the house.

Milia's eyes were red and swollen, she sniffled towards the girls. "Miss Serena, you must protect Aimee and the baby."

Aimee began to say something, but Serena jerked her off the chair. "Milia is right. We need to leave and recoup."

Aidan and Gamble jumped up to Serena's side. "We will come with you."

Serena shook her head. She did appreciate the gesture. "No, you boys need to stay here and watch Erik. With Nyx here, he will need someone he can trust."

Aimee ripped her arm away and planted both feet firmly against the grass. "I am not going."

Placing both hands against Aimee's cheeks and giving them a squeeze, Serena gave her friend a weak smile. "I know you want to fight. This is not the time or the place. I promise you: they will pay for what has happened. "

With the help of the boys, Serena pushed Aimee back into the Sanctuary. She practically had to drag her friend the entire way up the stairs. *What a stubborn elf.* Serena's heart raced, and she shoved open the elf's room. "Pack as much as you can. We need to leave quickly."

Aimee nodded. "Yes, yes. Go get your things."

Serena rushed to her room, pulling out the purple back-pack from the closet. She quickly shoved as many things as possible into it.

From the hallway, she heard Aimee scream.

Serena grabbed her backpack and rushed out of her room. Henrik had a fistful of Aimee's hair, and she shrieked as he dragged her across the hallway floor.

"Do you really think I would let some elf run around telling everyone about her bastard child? Trying to convince everyone it's my dead son's blood?"

Serena slammed the bag down into the ground. She lunged towards Henrik, resting her sword against his throat. "Let go of her hair, unless you would like to lose your head."

The rounds of Henrik's cheeks flamed. "You aren't very smart, attacking an Elder. If you let me have this filthy elf, I will spare your life."

With the edge of her hilt, Serena slapped him in the face. "I won't say it again. Let her go. I don't negotiate with psychopaths."

He loosened his grip and pushed her head away. "Go to your room and grab your bag. I'll meet you at the mirror portal." Aimee nodded without any hesitation and ran towards her room. The sword dug deeper into his throat as drops of blood began to trickle down his neck. "I should kill you for what you did to your sons and wife."

Henrik pushed back as hard as he could, slamming Serena into the wall. "You should have killed me when you had the chance." He whipped around, punching her in the stomach. She stumbled back slightly but recovered quickly as she was trained to do. Serena put her head back and slammed her forehead down into his nose. Blood gushed out from it like a faucet after a sickening crunch.

"You little bitch, you broke my nose!"

"You deserve much more than this." She kicked him as hard as she could between his legs. Henrik hunched over. His body curled up in a ball on the ground, and he howled in pain.

Aimee ran into the hallway. "Go! GO!"

She picked up the backpack and ran down the stairs. Henrik's screaming voice resonated throughout the Sanctuary. "Erik, arrest them. Don't let them escape!"

Loud thumping came roaring from the hallway. Serena looked over to see Erik storming out of his room. Both girls reached the front entry, as she tried to catch her breath. "Run, Aimee. GO!"

Aimee yelled, "*Eldamar.*" The elf ran full force into the portal, reached her hand out and just as Serena's fingers grabbed hold, Erik yanked her backpack, pulling her backwards. *Shit.*

"Keep going, Aimee. I'll find you." With another jerk at her backpack, Serena slipped her arms out of the straps. Erik tumbled back.

"You are under arrest for trying to kill a member of the elder counsel."

She shook her head. "I love you, Erik. Always and forever."

Gripping the edges of Serena's dress, Erik pinned her against the wall. The warm tickle of his breath danced across her face, he pressed his lips as hard as he could against hers.

"Don't you get it? if I don't arrest you, Serena, they will hunt you down and kill you. If I don't stop loving you, you will die. This is the only way." The palm of his hand gently caressed her cheek. His fingers lingered across her lips.

As the tears rolled down her face, all Serena could do was nod. Her voice was filled with betrayal, it hurt even herself to speak. "J-j-just make it easier on yourself and arrest me. Just forget all about me and live the rest of your life with the person responsible for killing your brother. Coward!" The small bit of spirit left in Erik's eyes seeped away.

Huffing and puffing, Henrik ran into the front entry, barely glancing towards Serena. "Good job, son." With a slap across Erik's back, Henrik's chest inflated and he licked his lips towards Serena. "Half-breed, you will have fun rotting in the cells of Fengsel."

Erik slowly waved his hand in front of her face. "*Sove.*" For a minute. Serena's body fought the spell, before crumpling down to the ground, her eyes closed.

❧

"Mommy? What's happening?" Serena was back standing in the lavender fields. Ailsa rushed towards her, wrapping both tiny arms tightly around Serena's waist. As she looked down, Ailsa's body began to disappear. "Please help me, Mommy. Don't give up. Please don't forget about me."

She shook her head. "I will never forget you, I promise."

"Ailsa? Where are you? Ailsa?" Serena fell to her knees, tears burning down her cheeks. "I am sorry. I won't give up on you, Ailsa. I will make this right."

# PRONUNCIATION GUIDE

- Aesir- "Ice-ear"
- Alfheim- "Alf-Hame"
- Baldr- "BALD-er"
- Bifröst– "BEEV-roast"
- Einherja- "ane-HAIR-ya"
- Fenrir- "FIN-reer"
- Frigg- "Frig"
- Jotunheim- "YO-tun-hame"
- Loki- "LOAK-ee"
- Muspelheim- "MOO-spell-hame"
- Nidavellir- "NID-uh-vell-eer"
- Niffleheim- "NIF-el-hame"
- Odin- "OH-din"
- Svartalfheim- "SVART-alf-hame"
- Valhalla- "val- HALL-uh"
- Valkyries- "VAL-ker-ee"
- Vanir-"Van-ear"

# SPELL GUIDE

- Amar- To summon earth
- Åpne Veien- Guardian spell to make portal appear
- Aske- Turn person or object into ashes
- Bloomstre- To summon a flower
- Cuil- To resurrect person or animal
- Doltha- To hid one's true identity, Glamour spell
- Edra- To open a magically locked door
- Forover- Push object or person forward
- Forsvinne- To make person or object disappear
- Hele- Heal minor wounds
- Kvele- To choke
- Låse- To magically lock door
- Reflektere- Reflect spell
- Sakte Ned- To slow down person or object
- Sparke- To summon flame
- Sove- To make person or animal fall asleep
- Stilne- To silence someone
- Tafnen- To magically block portal
- Tenne- To summon white light
- Vann- To summon water

# SERENA'S CHOCOLATE CHIP COOKIE RECIPE

- 1 cup of butter or margarine
- ½ cup of brown sugar
- ½ cup of white sugar
- 2 eggs
- 1 tbsp. of vanilla or almond extract
- 2 cups of all-purpose flour
- 1 tsp of baking soda
- ½ tsp of salt
- 1 ½ cups of semi-sweet chocolate chips

1. Heat oven to 375°F.
2. In large bowl, beat butter, brown sugar and white sugar until fluffy.
3. Beat in eggs and vanilla until creamy.
4. In medium bowl, mix together flour, baking soda and salt.
5. Gradually blend into creamed mixture.
6. Stir in chocolate chips.
7. Drop from small spoon onto ungreased cookie sheet. Bake 10 minutes until golden brown.
8. Cool cookies on wire rack

# BALDR: THE GOD LOVED BY ALL

Baldr was the second son of Odin and Frigg. Brother to Thor and Hodr. The mischievous god Loki convinced Hodr to throw the spear at him, promising him that no harm will come. The spear pierced through Baldr's chest; the god died instantly. Odin and Frigg, heartbroken over the death of their son, banished Loki's only daughter Hel to live eternally in the underworld realm of Muspelheim. After the banishment of Hel, Loki stole the golden horn from the God Heimdall. The golden horn would allow entrance to Asgard. Before Odin knew that Loki stole the horn, he banished Loki to spend all eternity in Muspelheim.

# THE BATTLE OF RAGNAROK

The Battle of Ragnarok took place in Asgard. Loki, with the support of the giants, dark elves and dwarfs, led the attack against the Aesir gods. After, he killed the god Baldr and took the golden horn. Loki was angry that he was cast out of Asgard by Odin to live eternally in the underworld. He crossed the rainbow bridge the god Heimdall guarded. He stormed the gates with all the manpower of all the lower realms. Surtur, the guardian of Muspelheim, released thousands of demons to join Loki's war. Thor smashed Loki's serpent son with his hammer. Thor succumbed to the serpent's poison and died. Loki and the God Heimdall were killed in an instant as they pushed each other's swords in the others heart. Odin fought Loki's oldest son Fenrir with his mighty spear. The monstrous wolf devoured Odin before Odin died he speared Fenrir in the heart. The Demi Gods and demons fought relentlessly. Frigg was filled with sorrow over the death of Odin and her children released a powerful spell. The spell caused the mountains to turn into huge Golems.

The Golems killed all the demons, dwarfs and elves. Surtur filled with vengeance took his giant flaming sword and set all the realms a blaze. Frigg and the remaining Demi gods sacrificed themselves and turned into a giant ocean, killing Surtur and putting out the flames to the realms that hadn't rebelled. The Golems one by one laid down in front of the gates, only to come alive if any man or creature tries to come near. After the war the remaining gods and light elves created the order of the Elders. The Elders declared that from this day until the end of time, all races and their descendants who rebelled would be punished. They would become slaves or face eternal imprisonment in the depths of the underworld.

# ACKNOWLEDGMENTS

I want to thank my husband, Joel; you are my rock. Without your constant reassuring, I am sure I would have given up a million times. My wonderful editor Evelyn, you have pushed me beyond what I could have expected. My father and mother, for your insight and advice. My book cover designer Larch, you create beautiful work. Last but least, I want to thank the readers—I hope you enjoy the book, and I can't wait to journey into other worlds together.

# ABOUT THE AUTHOR

Born and raised in Canada, Tiki started working on the YA novel Daughter of the Night in 2016—the first book in the trilogy. Tiki has been married to her husband Joel for the past two years. She is a mother of two wonderful children, Aiden and Scarlett. When she isn't working on her writing, you can find her drinking coffee and eating sushi. In her spare time, she enjoys baking, reading fantasy books, and playing video games.

www.tikikos.com

COMING SOON

Daughter of Eldamar — 2018

Made in the USA
Monee, IL
13 December 2019

18566227R00098